"N

Beau Devereux shook his head to emphasize his words.

"No?" Lucinda looked down at the ribbon in her hand. "Do you mean you do not care for this shade?"

"Not with that hair." *Or those extraordinary eyes,* he added to himself. He reached down absently and fingered a bolt of lace.

"You require something out of the ordinary. Look here," he advised.

"Gold Brussels lace," Lucinda whispered in awe. "But do you think it quite the thing, sir?"

Dev's eyebrows rose slightly. "I would not suggest it otherwise."

Lucinda touched the cobwebby fabric. "It is so fragile."

No more fragile than you, my dear, he thought as with an effort he reminded himself yet again where his true duty lay.

WHAT LUCINDA LEARNED

BETH BRYAN

Harlequin Books

TORONTO • NEW YORK • LONDON
AMSTERDAM • PARIS • SYDNEY • HAMBURG
STOCKHOLM • ATHENS • TOKYO • MILAN

For my parents

Published May 1991

ISBN 0-373-31150-8

WHAT LUCINDA LEARNED

CHAPTER ONE

THE LEAVES in The Priory House's orchard rustled in the soft breeze. A few late apple blossoms floated down and nestled gently in Lucinda Neville's chestnut curls. But she ignored them and gazed only at the young man in front of her.

"Married!" she exclaimed. "What do you mean, Will, you must marry?"

Her companion lifted a haggard face. "That's what I'm trying to tell you, Lucinda. M'father's got us to point-non-plus this time."

"Sir Oliver? He's been gambling again?"

"Gambling? Hah!" Will groaned and drove his fingers through his hair so that the blond curls stood up alarmingly.

"Cards, horses, money-lenders, I don't know what else besides. If the estate weren't entailed, that'd be gone, too."

"Will! Not Ryland Old Hall?" Abruptly, Lucinda sat down beside him on the circular wooden seat beneath the old apple tree.

"As I say, that's entailed. It's not even the mortgages I mind, Lucinda. I can pay those off when I come into Grandfather Ryland's fortune."

"Of course. I'd forgot that he'd left it to you. Doesn't that help, Will?"

"I don't get it till I'm twenty-five and that's four years away. In the meantime, we must live."

"But..." Lucinda hesitated, her huge, pansy-brown eyes clouded. "I don't entirely understand these things, but can't you, well, borrow against your expectations?"

"Hah!" Will attacked his curls again. "How do you think m'father got the mortgages in the first place?"

Lucinda bit her lip. "There must be something you can do, Will. Lady Ryland..."

"My mother," said Will grimly, "has retired to her room. She'll see nobody but the quack. She'll do nothing but physic herself and succumb to the vapours whenever anyone tries to talk to her."

Lucinda knew Lady Ryland of old and wasted no more time in comment. Then, as she remembered Will's sister, she cried, "Belle! Isn't Belle due back from France? She's making her come-out, too, isn't she?"

"Much good that'll do her if m'father ends up in a Round House."

Lucinda gasped. "Is it so bad?"

Will nodded grimly.

"But what can we do?"

"I know what I have to do, Cinda. I told you. It's up to me and I've got to marry someone with the dibs."

"You don't want to get married, Will. You want to go to sea."

"Of course I do. I— Sorry, Lucinda, I didn't mean to fly up at you. But I have as much chance now of buying a commission as I do of becoming King. I've got to do what I can to save the family, and that means an heiress."

Lucinda looked thoughtful. "Do you have anyone in mind?"

"How could I? There aren't scores of heiresses here in Nether Wilden, you know."

"There is one."

"What do you mean?"

"Me."

"You?" Will gaped at her.

Lucinda's brown eyes twinkled. "Yes, I have my mother's fortune. She left it to me, you know."

"Cinda, this ain't a funning matter."

"I'm not funning. Will—" Lucinda jumped to her feet, and clapped her hands "—wouldn't it be wonderful?"

"Wouldn't what be wonderful?" He reached out and grasped her hands. "Do be still, Cinda. You give me the headache watching you bounce up and down."

"That's the answer, of course. Once Sir Oliver's creditors know you're going to marry me, they'll stop dunning him and you can pay them off with the settlements."

"Lucinda!" Will's blue eyes flashed and he stood up. "You're not to say such things, do you hear me?"

Lucinda opened her eyes wide. "Whyever not, Will? You aren't in love with anyone else, are you?"

"Of course I'm not."

"Well, I'm not, either. So that's all right."

"It is not all right!" Will bellowed. Then he flushed. "What I mean is—"

"And," Lucinda went on unheedingly, "you do like me, don't you, Will?"

"That's got nothing to do with it."

"Why not?"

"Dash it all, Lucinda, there's more to marriage than just liking someone."

"I should have thought that was sufficient." Lucinda fixed her enormous eyes on him. "What else, Will?" Mr. Ryland's hands strayed towards his hair but tugged desperately at his cravat instead. "Lucinda, it ain't proper to discuss such things with me."

"You discuss them with Papa, then." Lucinda placed her hand on his arm and looked up at him through her long, sweeping lashes. "Don't worry, Will. You'll see I have hit on the perfect solution. And it won't change anything, you'll see. I'll come to live at Ryland, but apart from that, everything will go on just as it always has."

Will Ryland had never been able to resist either that tone or that look. When, some fifteen minutes later, he left the orchard, he had agreed to discuss an engagement with Mr. Neville that very afternoon.

Lucinda walked down to the main gates with him. She stood on the stile and waved to him as long as he was visible across the field. Then she jumped down and turned back to The Priory House. Before she came in sight of the windows, however, she stopped and broke into a delighted pirouette, sending her skirts swirling about so that they knocked the petals from the tulips bordering the walk.

Cousin Ethelreda would say that was highly unsuitable behaviour for a young lady about to make her debut. But, thought Lucinda gleefully, I needn't worry about that anymore. Soon I'll be a married woman, and married women can do anything they like.

LATER THAT AFTERNOON, Lucinda was not surprised to be summoned to her father's study. Mr. Neville seated her in one of the deep tobacco-coloured leather armchairs. Then he took his own place behind the desk.

He looked out of the large casement window for a moment, then brought his gaze back to his daughter. "I understand," he began gravely, "that you wish to become engaged."

"If you please, Papa," Lucinda said, belatedly remembering that his permission was necessary.

Jasper Neville took up his enamelled snuffbox. "I had no idea," he remarked pensively, "that you cherished a secret tendre for Will Ryland."

"I've always liked Will." Lucinda looked warily at her father. She did not always appreciate Jasper's taste for irony.

"Quite so." Jasper flicked open the box and took snuff in one expert gesture. "I have told young Ryland that if you are of the same mind after your Season, I shall consent to the engagement being announced."

"But, Papa—"

"I do not think I can be described as a Draconian parent, Lucinda. But I cannot countenance your engagement to the only young man you know before you've had a chance to spread your wings."

"I shan't like anyone better than Will."

"At least you will have had the opportunity," replied Jasper calmly.

"But Papa, Sir Oliver—"

"Will has told me of his financial difficulties."

"If we keep our engagement secret, how will the creditors—"

"I am not without influence, my dear. I shall drop a few words in the appropriate ears. Things may be difficult for a while, but Will is not destitute, after all. I think he will find that matters improve."

Lucinda did not look entirely satisfied and Jasper continued, "If you do wish to consider yourselves privately engaged, I cannot, as I have already told Will, prevent you. I merely insist that you go to London and partake of all the Season offers. Afterwards, we shall see."

"Very well, Papa." Lucinda recognized the finality in her father's tone. "But what is to be done about Belle? Lady Ryland is having one of her turns. Will says she claims she cannot undertake the responsibility of launching Belle in these circumstances."

Jasper picked up a sheet of heavy, crested paper from his desk. "This is from Lady Grantham."

"She is Belle's godmother, I think?"

Jasper nodded. "She's also an old friend of Ethelreda's. Her daughter, Patience, is to make her come-out this year also. Lady Grantham has written both to me and to Ethelreda, saying that she hopes you girls will all become friends and that she and your cousin may share chaperoning duties."

"Then she is willing to sponsor Belle?"

Jasper looked thoughtfully at her. "I suspect," he said dryly, "that Lady Grantham has always expected to do just that."

Lucinda's brown eyes widened to their fullest.

"You know, my dear, that life for Lady Ryland has never been easy."

Lucinda looked wise. "I know. Sir Oliver and his gambling."

"It is not entirely Oliver's fault," Jasper said slowly. "His father's will was, I think, most ill advised. He left most of his fortune in trust for Will and a mere pittance to Oliver. Oliver had always felt that his father despised him. The will did nothing to increase his sense of responsibility."

Lucinda's mouth formed a soft O of surprise. Papa had never talked to her like this before.

"A will is a powerful document, Lucinda. I hope you keep that in mind when it comes to your own children."

Bright colour flooded Lucinda's face. "Ch-children?"

"If you are thinking of marriage, my dear, then children are a natural consequence, don't you agree?"

Lucinda's eyes fell. She had certainly never considered children. Will's and her children? Doubtfully, she shook her shining curls.

Jasper studied her silently for a few moments. Then he said gently, "Lucinda, your mother and I were given very little time together. But every minute of that brief allowance has been an enduring delight and comfort to me." He paused. "It is my dearest wish that you will find that joy in your own marriage."

Lucinda blinked back tears. Mama was only a faint, far-off memory to her. That Jasper should mention her now moved her daughter deeply.

"However," Jasper went on more briskly, "you have the whole Season to think things over, though from what Ethelreda says, quiet reflection does not come high on her list of activities."

Lucinda laughed. "Have you decided whether you will travel with us, Papa?"

Jasper sighed slightly. He touched the stacks of papers on the desk. "I fear..."

"Are those papers from the Cranford estate?" she asked rather hesitantly. Papa did not generally discuss his business affairs with her.

He nodded. "As you know, I am the executor. The old earl died two months ago. Then his elder son died in that terrible accident. Two successions in less than two years complicate matters enormously."

"And the new earl has not yet returned to England?"

"No, but I have written to him in Italy, and I am in hopes of hearing from him shortly. He also must be eager to expedite matters."

"He is not married?" Lucinda was thinking it would be rather a sad homecoming for the young man who had come to the earldom through the death of his father and brother.

"He is still quite young. I believe there was some talk of an attachment when he was in London two years ago, but as far as I know it came to naught."

"And you will wish to see Mr. Bunthorpe in his new post in London."

"Yes, indeed. He is doing splendid work there, but the need is great. We have a new governor for that hospice, too, and I must meet with him before too long."

"Yes, I remember. A gentleman, I think you said?"

"A member of the haut ton, in fact. I hope to get many more men and women of influence involved so that they may realize their social responsibilities. This new governor is a step in that direction."

"If his appointment means that you will hurry to London, Papa, then I shall be delighted to meet him."

Jasper smiled at her. "Now, Lucinda, I shall not permit Cranford's affairs to delay me any longer than is necessary. I shall hasten to Town, not to see a new governor, but to see you. After all, I cannot miss my only daughter's debut."

As she left the study, Lucinda felt very pleased with herself. True, Papa had not exactly agreed to the engagement, but he had not forbidden it, either. More significantly, he had talked to her just as if she had been a grown woman.

She wasn't a schoolroom miss any longer, Lucinda thought ecstatically. And it was all because she had had the notion of becoming engaged to Will—it had completely changed the way Jasper thought of her. Alone in the hall, Lucinda did another little dance of delight. What a good idea it had been to marry Will Ryland! She was so glad she had thought of it.

"Lucinda! Whatever can you be doing?"

Miss Neville stopped rather sheepishly as a middle-aged lady advanced upon her. Mrs. Ethelreda Cleeson was a tall, thin widowed lady, with a vaguely harassed air. This was produced by chronic absent-mindedness, a trait she tried unsuccessfully to combat by making endless lists. She had lost her husband early in her married life and had come to live at The Priory House soon after the death of Lucinda's mother.

"You know, dearest," she reproved, "you must try to behave with a little more decorum. Such hoydenish conduct would be quite unacceptable in Town."

Lucinda laughed. "I shan't do it in Town, cousin Ethelreda. It's just that I am so very happy."

"Well, that is a change." Ethelreda stared at her. "But I am glad to hear it. As I told you, girls are very often nervous before their come-out. But you will enjoy yourself once it all begins."

"I know I shall."

Mrs. Cleeson blinked. "And what has changed your mind so much?" She looked back at the study. "Has Jasper been talking to you? I told you you need not worry. You do not like the idea of entering the Marriage Mart, but your papa would never coerce you into a marriage against your will. You need not be afraid of that, nor that he would reproach you should you not receive a suitable offer. Not," added Mrs. Cleeson, smiling at her charge's vivacious face, "not that such an event is in any way likely."

Lucinda chuckled, a deep husky sound. "No, I'm sure Papa won't reproach me."

Mrs. Cleeson was still puzzled, but she was happy to embrace her niece's turn-about. There could be no profit or pleasure in conducting an unwilling charge through the Season.

"Come upstairs for a moment, my love," she said, taking advantage of Lucinda's mood. "I have just received some new magazines. There is a ball gown I want you to see. I think if we were to have the sleeves altered..."

Lucinda spent a happy afternoon discussing fashions and fabrics. After dinner Will reappeared, and he and Lucinda strolled in the rose garden in the long twilight.

"Did you decide on settlements with Papa?" Lucinda leaned down to smell one of the early yellow blooms, so she did not see Will grasp a handful of his curls and tug ferociously.

"We—we didn't quite get to that."

"What did you talk about, then?"

"Your papa was advising me. He's already shown me several ways I might deal with the creditors—ways I'd never have thought of myself. After all, it's not as though I don't have any money whatsoever. I wish my father were as awake on these points as yours."

"I don't know very much about such matters, but I am glad that you feel happier about it."

Will shuffled his feet in the white marble chips on the path around the reflecting pool.

"And," Lucinda went on happily, "as he doesn't want us to make a public announcement yet, there's no hurry about the settlements."

With unnecessary violence Will kicked a stone into the still water. "Cinda, it's generous of you, dashed generous. But I can't take advantage of you like this..."

"Take advantage of me?" Lucinda echoed. "How could you possibly do that?"

"It's not that I don't appreciate it, Cinda, and I'll never forget it, truly I won't. But our plan ain't up to snuff and it's no good pretending it is."

"You've been listening to Papa."

"He's right, ain't he? I *am* the only chap you really know."

"You're forgetting the Bearley boys and there's John Gage..."

"Lucinda," said Will awfully, "if you are going to compare me to those spotty-faced, long-shanked..."

"No, no, naturally not." Lucinda giggled. "But Papa is worrying too much. You need not pay attention, unless—" her brown eyes clouded "—unless you wish to cry off?"

Will looked at the hurt in those dark velvet eyes, at the droop in the slight shoulders. "Ah, no, Cinda," he said impulsively.

Lucinda beamed at him. "Then that's all right. Now let's talk about London. Lady Grantham may sponsor Belle, so Papa tells me."

"Yes, she has written to Mama, asking both Belle and me to stay at her house in Cavendish Square."

"And will you?"

"I should think so, for, you know, it will spare me the expense of opening the town house and I shall feel much happier if Belle is directly under her eye."

"Don't you think that Paris will have calmed Belle down?"

"It'd take more than a few Frenchies to put a cramp in Belle's style. I went down to post a letter to her this afternoon. While I was in the village I met the new warden of the hospice. Edgely, his name is. I take it that you have met him already?''

"Yes, he came to dinner at The Priory last week.''

"Talkative chap, ain't he? Bent my ear for nearly an hour on what a good idea the whole hospice business was.''

"Papa is pleased with him, I know. But I do miss our dear Mr. Bunthorpe.''

"Doing well at the new hospice in London, I hear.''

"He's made a great success of it.''

"On the river, ain't it?''

"Yes, a most healthful situation, Mr. Bunthorpe says. It is essential for those who are ill to get out of the unwholesome city air. I do so look forward to seeing the new hospice and Mr. Bunthorpe, of course.''

Will grinned. "I didn't think there was anything in Town that you were looking forward to.''

She laughed happily. "Oh, there is! There is!''

"But just last week, you—''

"That was then. But now—'' she smiled at him "—now I feel quite differently.'' She frowned a little. "Not . . . not so *exposed*.''

Will looked rather helplessly at her. His hand crept towards his throat. He looked past her and breathed a sigh of relief. "Ah, here is Mrs. Cleeson come to fetch you in.'' He took her hand. "I thank you for everything, Lucinda.''

Shyly Lucinda smiled up at him. "I knew you could not really mean to cry off. For we are always the best of friends, are we not?"

Mr. Ryland made the only reply he could. "The best of friends, Cinda. Always the best of friends."

CHAPTER TWO

JASPER NEVILLE was not one to puff off his consequence, but he was well aware of what was owed to him and his daughter as members of one of the county's oldest, and wealthiest, families. Thus it was some three weeks before the arrangements and the entourage deemed necessary for Lucinda's departure could be completed.

At last all was in readiness. Two outriders, liveried and mounted on matching greys, led the voyagers. Behind them came the large and luxuriously appointed travelling chaise with the Neville arms emblazoned on the doors. Then followed a coach containing Emmie, Lucinda's maid, Albert, her footman, and Mrs. Cleeson's abigail. They all peered rather apprehensively at the mountain of boxes and baggage strapped precariously to the roof of their vehicle. The rear was brought up by another liveried rider. On a big, spirited black, Will waited beside Lucinda, who was in the first chaise.

Jasper was giving last-minute instructions to the coachmen. Both looked rather nervous, as it was the first time either had been to London, or indeed, beyond the nearest market town.

A list in one hand and an overstuffed reticule in the other, cousin Ethelreda bustled distractedly from carriage to carriage and back to the house. Mr. Neville finished his instructions to the drivers, then waited patiently for his cousin.

"Now, Ethelreda, permit me to repeat: when you reach London, you will come first to Agincourt Crescent, but you must continue—"

"Papa!" Lucinda leant out of the chaise, her face alight with laughter. "Papa, pray do not give your cousin Ethelreda any more instructions. She will be in the twitters altogether!"

Mrs. Cleeson half smiled, glanced down at the list and shrieked, "Mercy! I haven't checked those pillowcases!" She darted off.

At length, however, Mrs. Cleeson was installed beside Lucinda. The last goodbyes were said and the cavalcade set out. Nether Wilden and its village fell behind. The chaise rumbled down the country lanes and out onto the main road. The fields and hedgerows slipped by till it was time for lunch.

They stopped at a pleasant little inn, where a private parlour had long since been bespoke for them. Mrs. Cleeson called Emmie and Albert together and they huddled over yet more lists.

Will and Lucinda stretched their legs in the inn's small garden.

"I find the journey extremely wearying," Lucinda confessed. "It is tiresome to be cooped up inside like this."

"I should think it would be," agreed Will, "especially for you. I'll wager you wish you were on horseback, too."

"I certainly do," said Lucinda fervently.

"But even for a horsewoman like you, it wouldn't be at all the thing."

"I suppose not. But this is the longest journey I have ever made in a chaise, you know. I really do not care for it."

"But, Lucinda, I am afraid that we have still a considerable distance to go."

"Pray do not remind me! I shall be tempted to climb up behind you on Black Shadow."

Will laughed. "I should like to see Mrs. Cleeson's face if you did. But, speaking of horses, have you heard yet what happens to Mountmellor's stables?"

"No." Lucinda sighed. "As soon as the will is probated, Papa says he will be able to discover who the heir is. So we have just to be patient until then. But I do wish I knew just what is to become of Castor and Pollux."

"They're magnificent beasts," Will said as they went in to eat. "Whoever gets 'em is bound to look after 'em."

"I do hope you're right."

The inn's cook had made a very special effort and the table was crowded with a variety of delicious choices, including cold boiled beef, pigeon pie and several roast capons. But Will was the only one to do justice to the meal. He declared it a capital spread and eagerly set to. Mrs. Cleeson nibbled without much attention as she studied her lists and Lucinda was too excited to eat more than a few slices of chicken and some strawberries.

Afterwards they renewed their journey. For a while Lucinda's interest in the route held. She peered out of the window, watching for signposts and marker stones, remarking on the passing traffic and enquiring as to which village that church spire over there might belong to. But gradually she grew quieter and sank back against the squabs.

"Are you quite well, my love?" Ethelreda looked anxiously at her.

Lucinda pushed back a curl from her damp forehead. "It is so very hot," she fretted, "and I think I am getting the headache."

Cousin Ethelreda produced a bottle of rose-water from her bulging reticule. She sprinkled a few drops on a handkerchief and pressed it to Lucinda's forehead. "You are very hot, dearest," she murmured. Next she reached beneath the seat. She pulled out a basket and extracted a bottle, wrapped in damp newspapers. "The lemonade is still cold." She poured some into a glass. "Here, Cinda, see if this helps. The dust does dry one's throat so."

Lucinda drank eagerly, then lay back again. She moved her head irritably. "How much further must we go, cousin?"

Mrs. Cleeson's anxiety increased. "We have just come out onto the London road, but I fear we have a good four hours before us yet. I do hope, dearest, that you will not suffer from travel sickness."

But as the hours wore on, this proved a vain hope. By the time John Coachman had turned onto the crowded city streets, Lucinda's head throbbed incessantly. The dust seemed ingrained in her very pores and her eyes smarted. Each jolt and bounce of the chaise racked every bone in her body.

"How much further, do you think, Will?"

Riding beside the chaise, Will turned his head at Mrs. Cleeson's question. "I couldn't undertake to say, Mrs. Cleeson. We're only on the outskirts and traffic is very heavy."

Ethelreda looked out at the great variety of vehicles crowding the road beside them. "So I see. But I cannot be at all easy in my mind about Lucinda. We must get her to bed as soon as possible. Do, pray, urge John Coachman to hurry."

"I will ask him," Will agreed, but to himself he thought that the driver had all he could handle in this, his first experience of city traffic.

Ethelreda took Lucinda's hand. "Only a little while longer, my love. Try to be patient."

"If only the noise would stop," Lucinda muttered fretfully. "If only I might be quiet."

Doubtfully, Mrs. Cleeson glanced out of the window again. Now that they were within the city limits, the noise from the grating of iron wheels had increased enormously. "Soon, dearest, soon," she said soothingly, but she looked up eagerly when Will appeared at the window.

"We're in Piccadilly now, Mrs. Cleeson. Agincourt Circle is quite close, is it not?"

"Dear me, Will, I collect it is so. I was in London some years ago, but I have not stayed in that house since I was a girl. I could not find it now after all those years." She frowned. "Now, wait a moment. Was not Jasper trying to tell me something about Aginc—"

"Cousin Ethelreda, cousin Ethelreda," Lucinda tossed on the squabs. "I feel so very sick. Couldn't I get out, leave the chaise for just a moment, please?"

"Is that possible, Will? An inn perhaps?"

John Coachman shouted and Will followed the direction of his wave. "Ah," he sighed thankfully. "It's all right, ma'am. It's all right, Lucinda. We're here. We're at the right street. The coachman's seen the sign."

"Thank heavens!"

Lucinda opened her eyes. "May I get out now?"

The carriage lurched suddenly as it swung round a corner. Lucinda moaned and fell back.

"What is it? What is it now?"

"It's the second carriage, Mrs. Cleeson. He took the turn too sharply. Some of the boxes have fallen off. I must go to help them."

"But Lucinda, she must..."

"We are at Number 25 already now, ma'am. The servants will be out directly. The boxes are blocking the roadway. We must clear them before we have trouble with the watch."

"Please, cousin Ethelreda, let us get out. I cannot bear it any longer."

"I see lights inside," Mrs. Cleeson muttered. "But the door is still closed. They cannot have set anyone to watch for us."

Lucinda pressed her hands to her temples. "Shall we never be out of this dreadful carriage?" she demanded, her voice rising.

"Yes, yes, dearest, this very minute. Here is John Coachman with the steps. We shall dismount directly."

INSIDE 25 AGINCOURT CRESCENT, three gentlemen were just finishing dinner.

"Unfashionably early," the host, Mr. Richard Devereux, remarked. "But Charles has just come up from the country and I feared he might starve if we forced him to wait for Town hours."

The rather heavy-set young man beside him laughed. "I'm grateful to you for setting aside your scruples, Dev."

The eldest of the three men pushed the port decanter along the table. "So am I, Ricky. I'll eat one of your dinners, my boy, any time you care to serve 'em, and as for your wine—" he held a crystal goblet up to the light from the candles "—well, I'll get up from my deathbed for that."

"An eventuality that is far in the future, I trust." His nephew filled his own glass. "You're in no danger at the moment, I suspect. You would never miss a Season."

"I enjoy myself, neffy. I'm not as cynical as you, or as romantical as Charles here."

"Romantical?" Sir Charles Grantham spluttered indignantly as he reached for the port decanter. "What do you mean, romantical?"

"It's all those plays you see, Charles. They can't help but have an effect. For instance—" Dev shook his head mournfully "—I notice that you have taken to wearing your hair à la Kemble in last Season's Hamlet. It does for the stage, my dear fellow, but not, I assure you for London drawing rooms." He closed his eyes and said in a faint voice, "If you do not care for vintage port, Charles, I have some mediocre claret you may brandish about if you wish."

"Great heavens!" Ivor rescued the decanter and set it reverently down. "Didn't anyone ever tell you, push, don't lift port?"

Sheepishly, Charles apologized, then went on, "But, truly, Dev, are you not looking forward to the Season?"

Richard raised one straight dark brow and his air of well-bred boredom increased. "When you have seen as many Seasons as I have, Charles, you too will become a trifle weary."

"Had as many caps set at him, you mean, and held off as many matchmaking mamas," Ivor put in with a grin.

His nephew frowned at him but Ivor continued irrepressibly. "I don't doubt you're a catch yourself, Charles, but you can't compare with Beau Devereux."

"I shouldn't try," said Charles frankly. "But is that really why you don't enjoy the Season, Dev?"

"It's why he won't enjoy this one."

"Ivor," said Richard gently, "haven't you ever heard that good wine is best appreciated in silence?"

"I don't suppose you enjoyed much silence with m'sister Melpond."

Richard's lips twitched, and his rare, charming smile lit his face. "How did you know my aunt had visited me?"

"Told me she was goin' to. Wanted me to come along as well."

"Did she indeed!"

"Now don't fly up in the boughs, Ricky. I told her I wouldn't interfere. Not my affair—not hers, either, if it comes to that, but Melpond never could mind her business."

"My aunt was quite right," said Richard calmly.

Ivor choked and wine splashed on his waistcoat. "Demme, boy, don't say things like that when I'm drinking. Hang it, how could Melpond be right?"

"Her luck has to change sometime."

"Come now, Ricky, be serious. You can't have agreed with her. Dash it all, Charles, you tell him. He can't have agreed with her."

Sir Charles's bewilderment increased. "I don't quite . . ."

"Parson's mousetrap," said Ivor succinctly.

"Married? You, Dev? *Married?*"

Richard regarded his guests through his monocle. "Your enthusiasm touches me deeply, my dears."

Sir Charles flushed. "I say, I didn't mean, that I never—"

"Means he never thought to see you under the cat's foot." Ivor was unrepentant. "Never thought to see it myself."

"If you'd done your duty years ago, Ivor, you'd now be surrounded by a parcel of brats and my aunt would not be hounding me to save the family line."

"Never one for the petticoats, neffy," Ivor replied with a chuckle. "But tell me, have you any particular gel in mind, or are you waitin' to see the current crop?"

The eyebrows rose. "A schoolroom chit, Ivor?"

"No, not the thing at all. Sorry I mentioned it. What's it to be, then? A widow? Not too old, but with—"

"You are incorrigible, Ivor."

"Well, if you don't have a preference, I'll wager m'sister Melpond does. Who's she backing?"

"You are becoming excessively vulgar, my dear," Richard complained; nevertheless, he answered. "If you must know, Lady Melpond favours Lady Chloris dePoer."

"Lady Chloris dePoer!" his guests echoed.

"I am glad," drawled Richard, "to see how my aunt's choice meets with your whole-hearted approval."

"An accredited beauty, of course," Ivor said hastily. "But dash it . . ."

"But," Sir Charles began, "don't they call her..." His voice trailed off.

"The Ice Queen?" Dev supplied calmly. He cracked a walnut, easily manipulating the elaborate gold cracker with one hand. "Not a bad title for a wife, don't you think?"

Sir Charles blinked, but Ivor nodded wisely. "So that's the way of it, then—an arranged match. Aye, Chloris dePoer might well do for that—beauty, breeding, fortune, she's got 'em all."

"Just so." Dev's boredom was barely concealed.

"Chloris dePoer?" Sir Charles was frowning. "I'm trying to think. When I first came up to Town, wasn't there talk of a match between her and..."

"The younger Cranford." Ivor nodded. "They were making a book on it in White's. Thought it was a sure thing."

"So it never came to anything?"

"Dropped fifty guineas over it myself. Their fathers had some kind of falling-out, I heard. Don't know about what. But all the Cranfords have tempers to match their hair and dePoer's immovable once he gets a maggot in his head."

"But the old earl died, didn't he?"

"Aye, and the next son, too. Young Rollo's the earl now, but he's not come back to England yet, that I've heard anyhow. How about you, Ricky?"

His nephew shrugged. "Not that I've heard. Must you rehearse this ancient gossip, Ivor?"

"Good Lord!" A thought struck Ivor. "I suppose you'll give up this charity start of yours when

WHAT LUCINDA LEARNED   31

you marry. A female ain't likely to hold with your putting all that time, not to mention blunt, into such notions. I warn you, Ricky, there'll be no bearing Melpond if she thinks she's managed that."

"I haven't offered for Lady Chloris, Ivor, and should I do so, I see no reason why I should rearrange my life. Naturally I shall pursue my own interests as usual. But I repeat, at the moment I have merely agreed with my aunt that it is time I considered a suitable alliance. Lady Chloris is an unexceptionable choice."

"Rather you than me, neffy." Ivor caught sight of Richard's face. "Oh, aye, aye, boy, I was about to say I'd as lief embrace an icicle, but I'm mum, I'm mum."

Richard changed the subject by turning to Sir Charles. "Lady Grantham and your sister are safely arrived?"

"Yes, indeed. But you know how my mama dislikes travel. She's taken to her bed, with Patience to feed her thin gruel."

"Miss Grantham makin' her come-out this year?" Ivor asked. "Remember her when she was just a slip of a girl."

"She is, and my mama is also bringing out her god-daughter, Miss Ryland."

"That's Oliver Ryland's gel, ain't it? Heard he's under the hatches again. Finally done up. Though I did hear something about his coming round after all, didn't you, Ricky?"

Mr. Devereux had been staring absently into his empty goblet. "Oliver Ryland? He hasn't had sixpence to scratch with since I've known him."

"I've heard talk of his son's marrying an heiress."

"Will Ryland?" asked Charles. "I know him, but I'd heard nothing about a match."

Dev stood up. "There's some brandy in the library I'd like your opinion on, Ivor. I'll even risk some on you, Charles, provided you promise not to hurl it about."

They followed him into the hall. Loud knocking sounded from the front door and Larrigan, the butler, passed them with an expression of outrage on his face.

The three men entered the library. They settled themselves in the deep wing-chairs and Ivor propped his feet on the gleaming brass fender. But scarcely had they lifted the heavy snifters when a further to-do broke out in the hall. Dev's eyebrows rose. In one fluid movement he raised himself and strode out.

The others exchanged glances and then followed. Prudently, however, Ivor tossed off the last of his drink and stopped for a refill before going into the hall. There, a most unusual scene greeted them.

The butler stood barring the front door. Behind him peered two staring junior footmen. A number of housemaids clustered near the servants' door at the end of the hall.

"I tell you, ma'am," the butler was saying, "I tell you this is not..." He fell to one side when he saw Mr. Devereux approach.

Dev beheld a middle-aged lady, her hat awry, standing determinedly in his doorway. She supported a drooping figure, wrapped in a dark, hooded travelling cloak. As he stepped forward to speak, this figure raised its head.

He found himself staring into a pair of the largest, pansy-brown eyes he had ever seen. For a long moment their gaze held. Then a curiously glazed look swept over the great eyes. The translucent eyelids fell and he reached out just in time to catch Lucinda as she fainted.

CHAPTER THREE

LUCINDA OPENED HER EYES and gazed at unfamiliar faded pink silk walls. She could hear the dull rumble of metal wheels on cobblestones. In the background she could just make out someone shouting. Straining her ears, she deciphered the street-hawkers' cry: "Mackerel! Fresh mackerel!"

"I am in London," she said aloud and sat up.

As if on cue, the door opened and Emmie came in carrying a tray. Behind her bustled Ethelreda, her arms full of flowers.

"So delightful," she cried, "and on your first day in Town, too!"

"But are they for me?"

"Who else, child, who else? Now, Emmie, you can just leave the chocolate there."

Lucinda picked up the smaller of the two bouquets, a mass of tiny yellow roses. She read the card: "May these speed your recovery and help you enjoy London." It was signed "Charles Grantham."

"Sir Charles is dear Amelia's boy. I have not seen him for some years, but he has grown into a handsome man. But do look at these." Mrs. Cleeson indicated the great sheaf of white French lilacs.

Their heady scent enveloped Lucinda as she took them. There was no message, just the signature "R. Devereux" in firm black script.

Ethelreda smiled in satisfaction. "So thoughtful of them both. And, my dear, such a lucky thing for you, to have met Beau Devereux already. There is many a beauty who would give her eye-teeth to gain his notice."

Lucinda had a sudden vision of clear grey eyes under straight black brows. The blood rose in her cheeks and she buried her face in the cool white blossoms.

"And it was all my fault, even though the ending was so propitious. It is my wretched memory. I cannot tell you how many times Jasper tried to drum it into my head that it was Agincourt *Circle,* not Crescent. Yet when it came to the point, I completely forgot. I was never so mortified." Mrs. Cleeson flushed. "I know I was here as a girl, but I could offer Will no assistance and so we found ourselves at the wrong house."

"The wrong house?" Lucinda lowered the flowers. "We went to the wrong house? I seem to recall knocking, but I don't remember much of this Mr. Devereux and—" she glanced at the card "—nothing of this Sir Charles."

"No, dearest, you wouldn't. When I realized my mistake, I was ready to sink. But you had already fainted—small blame to you, my love—and Mr. Devereux immediately carried you inside to the library. He called his housekeeper, a most superior

person and then he and the gentlemen retired. The
housekeeper burnt some feathers to bring you round
and then she gave you a few drops of laudanum."
Mrs. Cleeson looked guiltily at Lucinda. "In general,
you know, I do not approve of such drastic mea-
sures, but you were so very unwell, dearest."

"So that's why I don't recall very clearly. How did
I get here?"

"A sedan chair! Yes, you may very well stare. It
seems Mr. Devereux keeps one for the use of his
grandmother, and both he and Sir Charles assured
me it was the very thing for you. You do not recol-
lect the gentlemen because of the laudanum." She
felt Lucinda's forehead. "How do you go on now,
Lucinda? Perhaps a day in bed . . ."

"Oh, no!" Lucinda threw back the bedclothes.
She jumped lightly to the ground and ran to the
window. "With London just outside, cousin, I
couldn't possibly stay in bed."

"Lucinda! Come back from that window at once!
The very idea! And you in your nightgown, too!"

Laughing, Lucinda obeyed. "Come, what shall we
do today, cousin Ethelreda?"

"There is no shortage of things needing to be
done." Ethelreda looked doubtfully at her. "We
must visit the modiste to order your gowns. I trust we
shall be able to find some ready-made till your own
are finished. Then you will require shawls, slippers,
boots, gloves, ribbons, fans—oh, hundreds of
things. And we must also consider the house. Jasper
has not used it for some years and it is in sad need of

refurbishing. We cannot hold your come-out ball until all that is finished. Oh!" She clapped her hand to her forehead.

"What is it, cousin?"

"I declare, I am more forgetful than ever. Amelia Grantham has written this morning to ask if we would attend what she calls an informal supper to-night. Though," Mrs. Cleeson continued, wrinkling her brow, "I should think she must have her hands full at the moment, for, you know, as well as her own son and daughter, she has Will and Belle staying with her. Perhaps we should not add—"

"Do say we may go, dear cousin. It would be so flat to spend our first evening in London at home. Besides, I long to see Belle again and I should also thank Sir Charles for his flowers."

"We-e-el, I really don't know that . . ."

"I feel quite positive, so do you write accepting immediately and I shall get dressed, then we will go out and see the Town."

Still vaguely protesting, Mrs. Cleeson departed. Lucinda rang for Emmie, and with her help was soon arrayed in a pretty lemon sprigged-muslin with an apple-green spencer. It represented the epitome of the village seamstress's work. Town ladies, Lucinda felt, would naturally wear something much more à la mode. But in this ensemble, at least she need not feel too much of a country dowd.

Ethelreda was, however, still more uneasy over Lucinda's health than over her wardrobe. "We really must not go racketing all over London and then go out to this party tonight. If you will not rest, then I must insist on a very small, quiet expedition, perhaps to one of the bookshops—"

"Let's go to Hatchard's, then! We may hand in Papa's list, as well as our own. What fun it will be to see the newest novels right away and not be obliged to wait till they make their way to Nether Wilden."

Ethelreda might have thought Hatchard's an unexciting little excursion, but she had reckoned without her charge's reaction to her first view of Town and her first sight of The Mall.

"So many people!" Lucinda hung dangerously out of the carriage window. "Where can they all come from? And, cousin Ethelreda, do look at that man over there. Whatever is he wearing?"

Mrs. Cleeson took a quick look. "Those are Petersham trousers, my dear. Only the veriest macaronis wear them. They are very wide, are they not?"

"Astonishingly so, and oh, do look over there—"

"Lucinda." Ethelreda took firm hold of her cousin. "You must sit down. Quite apart from it being excessively unbecoming, it is dangerous to lean your head out of the window in that way."

A gleaming black brougham dashed past them, almost grazing their wheels, and provided Lucinda with a graphic illustration of the truth of this dictum. So she reluctantly sat back and waited till they drew up in front of the famous bow-window.

There was a great coming and going at the front door of Hatchard's. The crowd seemed to Lucinda to be dressed in the first stare of elegance, and as they all seemed also to be the very best of friends, Lucinda felt a little shy and hung back.

However, Mrs. Cleeson was less intimidated and quickly shepherded her charge inside. They were immediately greeted by a clerk in the livery of the establishment.

He received Lucinda's lists with a deep bow, then indicated a large table, which seemed to be the centre of attention. "If you care to wait, madam, while your order is filled, the very latest volumes are displayed here. However, if you prefer, we shall deliver your order later today."

"Oh, no! We are going to look round, aren't we, cousin?"

Mrs. Cleeson's eye had already been caught by a large virulently green-coloured book, proclaiming itself *A Compendium of Infallible Herbal Remedies.* She nodded absently.

Lucinda eyed the ladies and gentlemen at the table. They all appeared frighteningly sophisticated, but they also demonstrated a complete lack of interest in her. So she plucked up her courage and reached out for a book.

The Season, she understood, did not officially begin for a week yet. But as she eavesdropped on the surrounding conversations, she heard constant references to routs, card-parties, breakfasts and receptions. A number of persons spoke of Lady Hoxborough's ball. It was, she gathered, *the* event to open the Season.

She sighed quietly to herself. She had never heard of Lady Hoxborough. In Nether Wilden she had known everyone and they had known her.

London was something quite different—and rather intimidating. But then she brightened. She had forgotten that she didn't need to worry about balls, routs, receptions and the like. It didn't matter what anyone in London thought of her. She was already engaged.

With this heartening thought, Lucinda plucked up courage, took three volumes and added them to the pile the clerk was amassing for her. She saw that Mrs. Cleeson was still immersed in her potions and set off to investigate other aspects of the shop. The books were mainly displayed on tall shelves which stretched from floor to ceiling and were arranged in very narrow aisles.

The books were packed tightly together on the shelves, and Lucinda could well believe the claim that volumes on every conceivable subject might be found here. Every few feet a protruding handwritten sign indicated the subject of the works in those cases. She grimaced as she saw that she was in an area devoted to sermons and quickly skipped round the corner.

There a large, somewhat tattered volume caught her eye and she was soon smiling over fashion plates of twenty years before. Surely no one had ever really worn her hair like that? So absorbed was she that she only gradually became aware of voices from the other side of the shelves.

"...always said it was a dammed silly notion, having a Circle and a Crescent with the same name. Scores of people get confused, I shouldn't wonder."

"Do you think so, Charles?" That was a drawl, a drawl so bored and uninterested that it set Lucinda's teeth on edge.

"Of course I do. Why, anyone might make such a mistake."

"Your innocence is refreshing, my dear. Experience will teach you that pretty young women and their matchmaking duennas make such mistakes only before the doors of the most eligible—and wealthiest—partis."

Lucinda froze.

"Come, Dev, I can't believe that, and if you do, why did you send her flowers?"

"Really, Charles. Miss Neville's behaviour may not be good ton, but mine invariably is. I am also somewhat acquainted with her father, who is of quite a different cut. Furthermore, I am loath to destroy your faith in womankind, but if I cared enough to bet, I should wager that Miss Neville will be more than happy to presume upon that very fortuitous mistake."

Lucinda snapped the book shut and shoved it onto the shelf. Her eyes flashed and two spots of colour burst in her cheeks. *Why, that opinionated, self-satisfied...*

She rounded the end of the shelves, ready to tackle the hateful Mr. Devereux. But only more rows of books confronted her. Aisles led off in various directions, but though Lucinda hurried down several, she found only a scholarly gentleman, perched atop a ladder, who frowned through his pince-nez at her.

Eventually she made her way back to the front of the shop. There cousin Ethelreda had abandoned her medicinal tome and was chatting animatedly with a rotund, red-faced gentleman. She beckoned Lucinda over.

"This is a very old friend of mine, Lucinda," she said brightly. "Someone I had not thought to see again. Ivor, this is my dearest Lucinda. Lucinda, this is Mr. Ivor Devereux."

Lucinda cast a smouldering glance at him, but it was obvious that this cheerful-looking stranger could not be the owner of that despicable drawl. She greeted him politely.

"Dashed pretty girl," said Ivor approvingly. "Glad to see you in better pin, my dear." He bowed over her hand. "I like a gel with high colour."

"Lucinda!" Mrs. Cleeson stared at her in consternation. "I hope you may not have overtaxed yourself. I knew I should never have permitted this outing. Ivor, I am delighted to have seen you again, but I beg you will excuse me. Come, Lucinda, your father will never forgive me if you are knocked to pieces before the Season has even begun."

Lucinda allowed herself to be bundled out of Hatchard's and into the carriage. She was still furious. How dared that man! To suggest she was set-

ting her cap at Beau Devereux! She, an engaged
woman!

She thought gratefully of Will. He would be just
as angry as she, were he to hear such imputations.
She settled back in her seat, her anger abating somewhat.

How fortunate that she did not have to worry
about what Mr. Devereux, or any Town beau,
thought. Ethelreda might be in alt at having met him,
but she was not on the Marriage Mart and she needed
no one's approval. When she saw him again, she
would show Beau Devereux just how little she cared
for his opinion.

THAT OPPORTUNITY presented itself sooner than
Lucinda had expected. She submitted to her cousin's fussing and spent the afternoon in bed, reading
one of her new purchases. Then she rose and dressed
leisurely in a favourite dress, a froth of cream over
mauve crêpe. It might be decidedly fuller than the
present style but it showed Lucinda's figure, particularly her tiny waist, to perfection. Emmie threaded
a matching velvet ribbon through her glowing curls
and tiny mauve rosettes decorated her white slippers.

The Grantham house was a tall, thin building in
Cavendish Square. Three ladies awaited them in the
front salon, two elegantly dressed young girls and a
plump matron with feathers in her hair. The latter
surged to her feet with a cry of "Ethelreda!"

While the two older women embraced, the younger ones had a chance to study each other. One was a quietly pretty girl with soft brown hair. But the other—Lucinda gazed in unfeigned admiration at the guinea-gold hair, the wide, china-blue eyes and the daringly low-cut gown.

This vision stared haughtily at her for a moment, then a mischievous smile curved the full red lips and one blue eye shut slowly in a wink.

"Belle!" Lucinda could scarcely believe her eyes. "Belle, is it really you?"

"Of course it is, you goose!" Belle hugged her.

"Let me look at you." Lucinda stood back. "I should never have recognized you. Paris has transformed you."

"Yes," said Belle with simple satisfaction.

The brown-haired girl spoke. "I'm Patience Grantham, Miss Neville. I think your cousin and my mama are too occupied with each other to introduce us now."

"So it appears. But do, please, call me Lucinda. I hope we shall all be friends."

"Of course we shall," agreed Belle. "For, you must know, Lucinda, that I have been telling Patience that we shall soon be all the crack. I am so fair, and your hair is so unusual and Patience is so pretty and gentle that we cannot help but become all the rage."

The other two girls laughed and Lady Grantham eyed them indulgently as she joined them. "That's good," she said. "I like to see young people enjoying themselves." She embraced Lucinda. "You are the image of your mother, my dear, and she too had that ravishing Titian hair. Now, where are those boys?"

Patience smiled. "You know, Mama, that they have gone to look at Charles's new horses. We shall be lucky if they remember us at all."

"Slander, Miss Grantham, I protest you slander us, and your own charms." Beau Devereux stood in the doorway. His bleu-celeste coat clung flawlessly to his broad shoulders; his buff pantaloons hugged his muscular calves. His linen dazzled in its whiteness, and in the folds of his intricately tied cravat, there nestled a huge pearl.

Lucinda heard Lady Grantham greet him and then Ethelreda thank him again for his assistance the night before. She recollected the words she had overheard him say in Hatchard's and clenched her hands.

"Lucinda dearest," said Ethelreda, beckoning. "I know you want to thank Mr. Devereux personally for his kindness."

Unhurriedly, Lucinda glanced round at the others. Will and a dark, stocky young man had just entered. The latter was modishly if rather flamboyantly dressed.

Beside the other two men, Will looked decidedly rustic. But as she watched him, Lucinda felt reassured and, lifting her chin, she went to Ethelreda.

A pretty enough chit, thought Mr. Devereux, mildly interested, *especially when she has a bit of colour.* He tapped a snuffbox with one long finger.

That hair is certainly remarkable. Then his attention sharpened.

Young ladies generally approached Mr. Devereux with downcast eyes or coy glances. He was not accustomed to being greeted by a lady with a martial glint in her eye and a combative tilt to her chin.

Lucinda looked coolly into those grey eyes. "I have to thank you, sir," she said in the closest imitation of his own tones that she could muster. "I fear we sadly disrupted your evening."

Cousin Ethelreda stared at her, but Mr. Devereux made a perfect bow. "Not at all, Miss Neville. I am gratified to have been of assistance." His voice held only polite interest, but was there the faintest lift to the corners of his mouth?

How dared he laugh at her? Lucinda inclined her head. "My aunt and I are most grateful for your help, sir, but I must not trespass on your indulgence any further. If you will excuse me, I must speak with Mr. Ryland."

She went quickly to where Will and Patience were sitting. Neither seemed to notice anything amiss in her manner, and she was glad to sit silently while Will recounted the virtues of Charles's new team.

Richard Devereux, she noted resentfully, did not appear snubbed. He was conversing with Belle, and to Lucinda's disapproval, that young lady was flirting shamelessly both with him and Sir Charles. She tried to concentrate on the conversation beside her, but her attention kept sliding back to the trio by the fireplace.

Fortunately the butler soon appeared to announce supper.

"As this is just an informal gathering," said Lady Grantham, "I am afraid that our numbers are not even."

"Then," said Richard, "I claim the honour of escorting you and Mrs. Cleeson."

"And I shall escort Miss Ryland." Sir Charles had eyes only for Belle and ignored his mother's minatory glance.

"I'm afraid that you ladies will have to be satisfied with me." Will offered an arm to Patience and Lucinda.

Once in the dining room, Lady Grantham took firm charge of the seating arrangements. Despite her son's obvious manoeuvres, Lucinda was seated on his right, beside Will and across from Patience. Sir Charles apparently easily recovered his temper and the four of them laughed and joked together very agreeably, though Sir Charles did display a tendency to glare up the table where Belle was endeavouring to monopolize Mr. Devereux's attention.

The Beau, however, was not so rag-mannered as to concentrate only on one lady. He divided his attention equally amongst Belle, Lady Grantham and Mrs. Cleeson. It was, Lucinda assured herself, only her own concern for Belle that made her, too, glance so frequently in that direction.

Still dubious as to Lucinda's state of health, Mrs. Cleeson insisted they depart soon after supper. As they left, Belle was gracefully posed on a gilt-legged sofa. Mr. Devereux sat beside her, his head bent towards her. On her other side, Sir Charles hovered frowningly.

"Your sister is marvellously changed," Ethelreda said in the carriage on the way home. Will had decided to escort them.

"Belle?" He spoke with brotherly unconcern. "She looks well enough, I suppose."

"Well enough!" Mrs. Cleeson was shocked. "I am sure Mr. Devereux thought her more than well enough!"

"Mr. Devereux?" Lucinda repeated sharply. "Surely you did not imagine that he was interested in Belle?"

"Shouldn't think he could be," Will answered. "The betting in the clubs is that he will offer for Lady Chloris dePoer before the Season's out."

"Chloris dePoer?" Mrs. Cleeson was intrigued. "That will be Melisande's girl. Yes, she would be the very thing—an excellent match for a Devereux. I remember the last time I saw Melisande and her..."

Her voice ran on in tangled reminiscences. Suddenly, Lucinda found she had a headache. What an insipid evening it had been altogether. And now, why was Will boring them with this trivial gossip from the men's clubs? It couldn't matter less to her whom Richard Devereux married. She was, after all, an engaged woman.

CHAPTER FOUR

LUCINDA SLEPT UNEASILY and awoke late. She had barely finished dressing when she was informed that Miss Ryland had called.

"Lucinda," Belle declared as soon as she saw her, "Lucinda, isn't he wonderful?"

Something seemed to have gone wrong with Lucinda's voice, for she opened and shut her mouth several times before she managed to mutter, "Wonderful?"

"I wish you could have stayed last night. Mama played for us and we were allowed to dance, even to waltz."

Lucinda had a sudden vision of Belle twirling in Mr. Devereux's arms. Hurriedly she sat down. "H-how delightful for you."

"Of course," Belle went on, holding out her yellow morning dress and waltzing dreamingly about the room, "he doesn't dance very well, but that doesn't really signi—"

"Beau Devereux can't dance?"

Belle stopped. "Of course Mr. Devereux can dance, and beautifully, too. But do pay attention, Lucinda, I am speaking of Sir Charles."

"Sir Charles?"

"Whatever is the matter with your voice this morning, Lucinda? It goes up and down astonishingly."

Lucinda laughed shakily. "I didn't sleep very well, Belle. Pray forgive me for being rather slow today."

"No, you must forgive me." Belle was contrite. "Patience said we must enquire whether you were fully recovered before we all descended upon you. But I quite forgot to ask."

"Belle!" Lucinda regarded her in exasperated affection. "Do you mean you have left Patience all alone in the carriage all this while?"

"Oh, Will's with her."

"What a wretched girl you are. I shall send someone out for her."

"No, don't do that. Send for your wrap instead. We've come to take you to Gunther's Pastry Shop, for, you know, it is the place to see all the ton."

"I must ask cousin Ethelreda first."

But Mrs. Cleeson had no objection. Planning a massive shopping expedition that afternoon, she was happy to have more time to refine her lists.

So Lucinda donned her bonnet, a fetching straw decorated with silk roses and primroses to match the embroidered bouquets scattered over her muslin round dress, and set off.

Will and Patience did not appear upset by their long wait, and they had a merry journey to Piccadilly. Lucinda actually recognized part of the route and was able to remark with tolerable casualness that she had picked up some interesting things at Hatchard's yesterday.

Will saw them into Gunther's and installed at a coveted window seat. Then he took his leave, declaring that he would not "maudle his insides" with sweet stuff at that hour of the day.

The ladies suffered no such compunction. Soon they were enjoying dishes of Gunther's famous pastel-coloured ices.

Belle had just put down her spoon when an imposing dowager in a formidable orange turban approached them. She was, she announced, a dear friend of Lady Ryland's and she bore Belle off to another table to interrogate her on family matters.

"You have known Belle and Mr. Ryland for a long time, I collect?" Patience asked in her soft voice.

"Forever," Lucinda replied as she regretfully finished off the last of her raspberry ice. "We are near neighbours in Nether Wilden, you know, and we have visited back and forth since we were children."

Patience looked wistful. "I should dearly have liked a little girl neighbour when I was growing up."

"Actually, I was more often with Will because, you know, Lady Ryland was away often and she took Belle with her when she went to Harrowgate or London or the like. I didn't mind that so much, but I was desperately lonely when Will went up to Cambridge."

"But he has been down for some time now?"

"It's been just like old times. In fact..." Lucinda paused for a moment. She did not want to bore Patience, but the other girl seemed more than just politely interested. "My papa at one time asked if I had removed myself entirely to Ryland Old Hall. He does like to tease sometimes."

Patience pushed her dish away. She hadn't finished her ice, Lucinda noticed. Perhaps the redcurrant ice wasn't as successful as the raspberry.

"You and Mr. Ryland are close friends, then?" Patience asked in a rather colourless voice.

"Oh, yes," Lucinda agreed fervently. Suddenly she was overwhelmed by a sense of her great affection for Will; simple, reliable, steadfast Will whom she'd known for as long as she could remember. "Oh, yes. I think Will must be my dearest friend."

"At last!" Belle returned and flopped into her chair. "After all that, I shall order another ice."

"That was Lady Hoxborough, I think?" Patience asked.

"A bosom-bow of my mother's, but I feel just as I felt at school when the headmistress quizzed me about the music master."

"The Hoxboroughs' ball is always the first of the Season. Shall we see you there tonight, Lucinda?"

"No, I think not. Cousin Ethelreda has not mentioned any ball."

"She will." Belle was tucking into her second ice. "When I told her who you were, she promised to send you cards right away."

"A ball!" Lucinda said excitedly. "But I don't think I have anything to wear to a London ball."

"Well," Belle pointed out reasonably, "you've got the whole afternoon to shop."

They had; but, as Lucinda soon discovered, they had need of every minute.

ONCE BACK IN AGINCOURT Circle, Lucinda partook of a quick lunch with her cousin.

"Belle said Lady Hoxborough is to send us cards to her ball tonight, cousin Ethelreda."

"The Hoxborough Ball! Good heavens, Lucinda, if we receive cards, then of course we must go. I know she is a friend of Lady Ryland's, but because we have just arrived, I did not expect— *When* did you say it was?"

"Tonight."

Mrs. Cleeson gave a little shriek and made a dive for her lists. "Then we must hurry. We cannot see about the house today. We must go at once to Célie's. Thank heavens you are not likely to be difficult to fit. At least I sent out yesterday to Paternoster Row, so you have new silk stockings. But the dress— Let us hope that Célie has something suitable already made up." She pushed back her chair. "Come along now, Lucinda, don't dawdle. I really do not know how we are going to find time for everything. Come along, come along, do!"

Lucinda did not know what to expect from a London modiste. But she was rather surprised when the carriage drew up before an unmarked house in a fashionable part of Town. An impassive manservant ushered them into a spacious first-floor reception room.

Lucinda looked round at the tasteful furnishings and the huge bowls of roses and pink lilies.

"Ah, Madame Cleeson!" A little lady with beautifully dressed white hair and a gown of dove grey arrived and grasped Ethelreda's hand. "So many years, I cannot believe it!"

"Nor I," declared Mrs. Cleeson with a laugh, "but those years have dealt kindly with you, Célie. And see, I have brought you my niece, Lucinda Neville, Jasper's daughter, you know. She is to make her come-out this year, and naturally you are to make her dresses. But now we are to go to the Hoxboroughs' ball tonight, and," she concluded dramatically, "she has not a thing to wear."

"*Là!*" Madame Célie threw up her hands, then came to stand before Lucinda. "*Lève-toi, s'il vous plaît, ma petite.*" As Lucinda rose, Madame Célie circled her, nodding. "*Bon, bon!* You have the *jolie forme, ma belle,* but very slight, so I think we shall find something. It will need *peut-être* a stitch here and there but we shall contrive, we shall contrive."

Lucinda was whisked off into a smaller room which seemed largely furnished with huge mirrors and small gilt chairs. She stood in her shift while Madame Célie and a succession of assistants popped an endless variety of gowns over her head. To her, they all seemed fairylike, but Madame Célie was less easy to please.

"*Oh, non! Pas ça!* Too many frills. Bring the other, the pale blue." Then, as that one was eased over Lucinda's curls, "*Non!* Not that one either—the colour is too insipid for such hair."

Lucinda's legs ached and she longed to sit down. But beyond asking her to raise her arms or turn about, no one paid any attention to her.

She was beginning to feel quite tired and rather irritated when Madame Célie at last said, "So, Madame Cleeson, you will take the *blanche et or* for tonight. A few tucks here and there and it will fit *à la merveille.* The other two we shall also adjust. I shall send them to you later this afternoon. Now do you and *la petite* take some tea and we shall then look at fabrics for the other ensembles."

Thankfully Lucinda resumed her own clothes and they returned to the first room where they drank pale China tea from exquisite paper-thin cups.

Madame Célie bustled in again, this time with pattern books and swatches of materials. For a while, Lucinda's attention was caught, but there were so many pictures, so many fabric samples and Madame talked so quickly and flipped the pages so rapidly, suggesting these sleeves here and that neckline there, adding lace here, a row of ruffles there, that at length she simply sat back and nibbled on a sweetmeat, leaving everything to her cousin and the modiste. On the rare occasions when they appealed to her, Lucinda merely nodded.

"Gracious, look at the time!" Mrs. Cleeson cried, suddenly coming back to reality. "We must go immediately, so you may have time to rest. Célie, I depend upon you for that white and gold gown for tonight. Now, Lucinda, let us go at once. Come along now."

It was all anyone seemed to say in London, Lucinda thought as she climbed back into the carriage: come along, come along, come along! And all she had done today was look at dresses. But she had never realized that shopping could be so exhausting. She was actually looking forward to the rest Ethelreda had decreed.

But later that evening, Lucinda had to admit that it had all been worth it. She turned slowly in front of the huge pier-glass.

Was it really her: the slender, perfectly gowned figure she saw reflected there? She studied the dress again—her first London model. It clung tightly to her bosom, then fell into a divided skirt of thin white silk over a pale gold underdress.

Tiny gold stars with diamonds in their centres sparkled in her hair and in her ears. A gauzy shawl, woven with gold and silver threads, was draped over her white shoulders.

"Excellent, dearest," cousin Ethelreda declared as she twitched one last shining curl into place. "Célie is always right. That gold colour brings out the glints in your hair and eyes. Come along now or we shall be late. Remember we promised to meet the Granthams."

Lucinda was grateful for this arrangement later. They met their friends in the hall of the Hoxboroughs' house in Eaton Square. The impassive liveried servants smoothly took charge of wraps and gloves and hats, then shepherded the guests into the receiving line on the first landing.

As she followed Mrs. Cleeson and the footman up the curving staircase, Lucinda felt quite lost. She had been to assemblies and young people's parties in Nether Wilden and the surrounding countryside. But nothing had even been as grand as this.

"Mrs. Cleeson and Miss Lucinda Neville," the footman intoned sonorously.

Lucinda felt so overwhelmed that she could scarcely raise her eyes to Lady Hoxborough as that formidable lady greeted Ethelreda.

"Jasper Neville's gel, eh?" her ladyship boomed and Lucinda caught a glimpse of figured green satin and a massive, if particularly ugly, collar of emeralds. "Looks just like her mother, and—" Lady Hoxborough bent towards Mrs. Cleeson and proclaimed in what was meant to be a whisper "—*and* a fortune to boot! You'll have your work cut out for you, fending off the bucks." She nodded as the scarlet-faced Lucinda bobbed a curtsy and passed her on to Lord Hoxborough.

Their host was a thin, self-effacing man, with a vague, unfocussed glance. He shook hands and murmured endlessly. "Welcome, delighted to see you, welcome."

Another footman threw open the doors to the great gilt-and-marble ballroom. Lucinda shrank back as she stared into the room where the floor-to-ceiling mirrors reflected the immaculately dressed members of the haut ton.

"Oh!" whispered Patience behind her. "It's all rather frightening, isn't it?" Miss Grantham wore a flattering shade of daffodil; nonetheless, Lucinda thought her pale.

"Frightening?" Miss Ryland scornfully repeated. Belle herself looked anything but frightened. An aura of elation surrounded her. She was in her best looks in a rather daring gown of blue-and-white stripes, with a coronal of white camellias surrounding her upswept curls. "Just wait till the dancing starts. Then we shall be too busy to be frightened."

Belle prove͏ true prophet and Lady Grantham and Mrs. Cleeson had ample opportunity to show their mettle as chaperons, for all their charges enjoyed a steady stream of partners.

The prospect of dancing before such a crowd had thoroughly unnerved Lucinda. But in such a squeeze, she soon realized, she was not likely to be the cynosure of all eyes. Once on the dance floor, amongst the other participants, she relaxed a little and began to take note of her sumptuous surroundings and to answer her partners in more than monosyllables. She was pleased she was able to identify some faces in the shifting press of people.

At the edge of the dance floor she caught sight of Will. He was gesturing animatedly, his face excited. A turn of the dance revealed his companion: Beau Devereux.

Lucinda's heart jumped and she lost the rhythm of the dance. Her gangly young partner blushed scarlet as she trod on his toe and began to stutter incoherent apologies. Guiltily, Lucinda devoted herself to him for the rest of the set.

But when she returned to the chaperons' corner, she looked eagerly about. With another stab of expectation she saw them coming towards her.

"Lucinda," Will called out to her. "You cannot guess!"

His enthusiasm was infectious, and Lucinda laughed a little as she clasped his hand, before turning to greet Mr. Devereux with a more correct, cooler smile.

The contrast rather piqued that gentleman, but before he could speak, Will rushed on. "Cinda, Mr. Devereux has Castor and Pollux!"

"You have, sir? I cannot tell you what a relief that is. We have been so worried since Lord Mountmellor died." And Lucinda beamed on him.

"Mountmellor was my godfather, Miss Neville. He left me his stables, including the horses you mention."

"We knew he had no family and we were so anxious..."

"Forgive me, Miss Neville, but why?" Lucinda and Will stared at him. Mr. Devereux smiled slightly. "I only received the horses last week. Any of their papers will have been sent to my place in Devon."

"So," said Will, "you haven't had a chance to look at their bloodlines sir? Lucinda's papa bred 'em, out of Jupiter. You'll have heard of him."

"Only their mother died just after she foaled," put in Lucinda. "We had to raise them by hand."

"When Lucinda says 'we,' she means *she* did. She even persuaded her father to let her sleep in the stable—with her maid, of course."

"I shouldn't think Emmie has forgiven me yet," Lucinda said, chuckling. "But they were so very tiny and they had to be fed every three to four hours, so it was quite absurd to be running between the house and stables all night."

"And Lucinda was the only one they'd either of 'em take the milk from."

"You seem to have a veritable knack for such animals, Miss Neville."

"She does, she does. Why, she's as good as the local horse doctor any day."

"Will," Lucinda protested. "Mr. Devereux doesn't want—"

"In fact," Will went on, unheeding, "if one of my cattle were sick, I'd as lief have Lucinda anytime."

Lucinda flushed. "Don't be absurd, Will. You know that I couldn't do surgery or the like and you must—"

"And she rides to perfection." Will was, it seemed, determined to boast of Lucinda's talents. "Firm seat, hands like a feather, able to manage the strongest horse, even though she looks like a little bit of a thing."

Mr. Devereux eyed Lucinda's slender figure. "I'm sure you are a famous rider, Miss Neville, but were you not dismayed when your father sold Castor and Pollux?"

"I saw them regularly at Lord Mountmellor's. But indeed I was greatly worried over what would become of them. I am glad to be reassured."

"Are you so sure they will be safe with me?"

Lucinda stared at Mr. Devereux, whip extraordinaire and member of the Four-in-Hand Club. Doubt flickered in her eyes. "W-what do you mean?"

Richard bestowed one of his rare smiles on her. "I am merely reminding you to take nothing for granted, Miss Neville. I shall indeed take good care of the horses, but you should enquire further." He held out his hand. "I shall submit myself to your cross-examination, if you will submit to the next dance."

Lucinda was so very far from availing herself of this permission that she said nothing at all for the first few moments of the dance. Belle was right about Mr. Devereux's dancing ability, she thought, her gaze resolutely fixed on the floor. Hitherto, she had been partnered by young men as green and nervous as herself. But this . . .

"Now, Miss Neville . . ." Mr. Devereux sounded amused. "I am sure those are charming slippers you are wearing, but you are permitted occasionally to glance at your partner, you know. Not even the strictest duenna would forbid it."

Lucinda chuckled. "Ah, but sir," she said, peeping up at him through those long, sweeping lashes, "if I were to miss my step, everyone would know it was my fault. For how could the accomplished Beau Devereux be so clumsy?"

To say that Mr. Devereux was enchanted would be too much. But he was amused—and a little intrigued. The little Neville, he told himself, was something out of the usual style.

In her endeavours not to stare too directly at him, Lucinda had been scanning the crowded dance floor. Now her glance focussed on a couple gliding by. Even in that dazzling company the woman stood out.

Her hair was of the palest gold, twisted elaborately about her head. Her white gown held only the faintest hint of green and she wore magnificent diamonds. Above all, however, Lucinda noticed her air of complete self-possession.

"How lovely," Lucinda breathed. "Who is she, do you know, sir?"

He followed her nod. "That is Lady Chloris de-Poer," he said evenly.

Lucinda's face grew crimson. *Oh no,* she thought, *not the woman he was supposed to marry!* "She's very beautiful," she managed to murmur, trying to appear cool.

"Indeed, she is accounted a diamond of the first water." His voice held nothing but casual interest. Then he went on, "Now, about those cattle you raised, Miss Neville..."

Lucinda was glad enough to change the topic, but all Mr. Devereux's easy conversation could not banish her sense of humiliation. So she was both relieved and obscurely disappointed when the dance ended and he led her back to cousin Ethelreda.

"Thank you, Miss Neville," he said making his effortless bow. "And, Mrs. Cleeson, I hope I see you well?"

"Indeed, sir," Mrs. Cleeson answered, all a-flutter. "So many people I haven't seen for so very long. It is quite a reunion for me."

"I shan't keep you from them, then. But I hope you and Miss Neville will permit me to call upon you soon."

"Why, of course, Mr. Devereux. We shall be delighted."

"Next time, Miss Neville, I hope I may show you the subject of our conversation—in the flesh." With another bow, he turned and melted into the crowd.

Gone to find Lady Chloris, Lucinda supposed. What a striking couple they must make—he so dark and she so fair. She became aware that cousin Ethelreda was speaking.

"... becoming quite chilly I think."

Privately, Lucinda found the room stiflingly overheated, but aloud, she said, "You must put on your shawl, cousin."

"Oh, dear." Ethelreda looked vaguely about. "I know I brought it with me."

"We were in the ladies' withdrawing room," Lucinda said. "Would you like me to see if you left it there?"

"So kind of you, dearest."

Lucinda threaded her way through the guests, nodding at those she recognized. Nowhere, however, did she see either Lady Chloris dePoer or Mr. Richard Devereux.

It was cooler and much quieter in the hall outside the ballroom. She knew the room was down the corridor on the left. But which door was it? She tried the first one.

It opened on what appeared to be a butler's pantry, and as she was reclosing the door she heard a scurry of footsteps. Glancing over her shoulder, she saw a wisp of pale green whisking around the end of the hall. Lucinda smiled indulgently. Had she interrupted an assignation?

The next door was the room set aside for ladies to rest or readjust their toilettes. There was cousin Ethelreda's Norwich shawl trailing over a sofa back. Lucinda gathered it up, but the long fringes had caught on the sofa's carved leg. As she bent down to free them, Lucinda caught sight of a glitter in the carpet.

It was a brooch, a pretty thing of citrines and diamonds. As she looked more closely at the white and yellow stones, she saw that the design comprised two interlinked initials. She traced them out with her fingers: C and R.

Lucinda sat back on her heels. C and R and a flash of ice green—Chloris and Richard. Chloris and Richard slipping away from the ball for a lovers' tryst, perhaps even to exchange this lovers' token.

Lucinda did not know how long she stayed there, crouching on the floor with the love-gift in her hand. It was a delicate little piece, but in her hand it became a lump of heavy ice. The cold radiating from it chilled her blood and numbed her heart.

"Ah, there you are, Cinda." Will stood at the door. "Mrs. Cleeson was worried when you didn't return."

Lucinda jumped hurriedly to her feet. She slipped the brooch into her reticule and reached for the shawl. "Here I am, Will. Let's go back to my cousin."

Lucinda had been carefully brought up. She would not dream of allowing anyone to guess at the turmoil in her mind. So as the ball continued, she danced, talked and went in to supper. But she could not forget those entwined initials. Now hidden in her reticule, the jewel had become a fiery torch, burning relentlessly into her thoughts.

CHAPTER FIVE

AT THE CORRECT HOUR next morning, Mr. Devereux presented himself in Lady dePoer's salon to take Chloris for a drive in his high-perch phaeton. He responded politely to his hostess's string of inanities, but his thoughts were busy elsewhere.

As he had told his uncle, his mind was not yet fully made up; however, his Aunt Melpond had given voice to a concern that had lately been growing in him. He was aware of his duty to his family, and that meant marriage.

He had enjoyed a number of liaisons with a series of expensive and extremely dashing high-flyers. He had conducted these affairs amiably and ended them equally so; after which, he had never given them another thought.

Any number of well-bred girls, beautiful and plain, wealthy and poor, clever and dull, had left him equally unmoved. But if he must marry, it was from the ranks of such women that he must choose— though he had never met one with whom he would care to spend the rest of his life.

But how many of his friends, he reflected cynically, *did* spend their lives with their wives? Didn't most of them pursue entirely separate interests, meeting politely when appearances demanded, but otherwise impinging upon their spouses scarcely at all?

It was, he thought, unaccountably nice in him to baulk at such an arrangement.

"Ah, here's Chloris now," said Lady dePoer.

Richard rose as she came towards him. She was dressed for driving, and when she gave him her hand, her manner deftly blended warmth and discretion. She gave no hint that she suspected he had any purpose beyond that of a morning ride.

She's very pale, Richard thought. *What she needs is a little of the Neville girl's colour. And what,* he asked, catching himself, *is the point of that very irrelevant comparison?*

He bowed over Chloris's hand. "Lady Chloris, I have persuaded your mama to entrust you to me for a drive."

"Why, sir," Chloris replied in her cool voice, "how could Mama be anxious when I shall be with such a famous whip?"

They took leave of Lady dePoer. As he handed Chloris into the phaeton, Dev considered her again. Her lemon-coloured driving habit was in excellent taste, her hat decidedly flattering and her whole manner precisely judged.

But, he asked himself, was there anything more to her than this perfect, doll-like surface?

LADY CHLORIS DEPOER also occupied Lucinda's thoughts that morning. She sat up in bed, sipping chocolate and eyeing her reticule. What was she to do with that brooch?

Should she send a footman to deliver it to Mr. Devereux? To Lady Chloris? Should she, perhaps, give it, herself, to Mr. Devereux the next time they met? But it was a love-token, something no outsider was meant to see.

Not yet, anyway, for no engagement had yet been made public. It would be embarrassing for everyone were she to thrust herself into the secret. If she were to send it to Lady Hoxborough, that lady would doubtless bruit it all over Town. Perhaps returning it anonymously to Mr. Devereux would be the best plan.

Should she show it to cousin Ethelreda? Mrs. Cleeson would certainly have some useful suggestions, but somehow Lucinda shrank from sharing her find with anyone else. She kept her thoughts about the brooch resolutely centred on how to return it, and she soon persuaded herself that she had no concern for doing so beyond the correct procedure.

"What, still in bed, dearest? You must not be late you know. You are to join Will and the others for a drive in the Park this morning."

Lucinda put down her cup and made to get up. She had quite forgot the arrangement they'd made last night.

"You might wear that new driving habit—the chocolate brown one—and the hat with the white feather, I think."

There is nothing like new, becoming clothes to cheer one up. As she sat beside Belle in Will's new sporting curricle, Lucinda felt quite pleased with the world. It was fashionable to ride in the Park at this hour, and she and Belle garnered quite a number of appreciative stares. She was even able to greet a selection of persons herself, and while these were not nearly as numerous as Belle's acquaintances, it gave her a gratifying sense of belonging.

After they had stopped for the fifth time, Will said good-naturedly, "Next time we had better walk. You girls seem to be on speaking terms with half the ton."

"Will!" Lucinda clutched his arm and pointed. "Look over there. What is that man doing?"

"Where? Ah, I see. The fellow with the two-wheeled contraption. I've only seen a few of them. They're called pedestrian curricles."

Lucinda watched fascinated as the man got up a little speed by running. Then, when the wheels of his curious vehicle were rolling swiftly, he put up his feet and coasted along till it was time to run again.

"Some people call it a Hobby-Horse bicycle," Belle said knowledgeably.

As they passed the vehicle, Lucinda saw the rider's face was red and shiny with perspiration. "It looks an awful lot of work," she said doubtfully. "I think I should prefer to walk."

"Look!" said Belle in her turn. "There's Mr. Stratton."

Lucinda watched the young man riding towards them. He was handsome in a rather showy way. Like his horse, Lucinda thought. Flashy, but she wouldn't be a bit surprised if that mount were touched in the wind. She had noticed Belle dancing with Mr. Stratton last night. Now, something in Belle's manner made her wonder if their meeting had been prearranged.

Mr. Stratton reined in beside them and swept off his high-crowned hat. "Ladies, Ryland, your servant. What a lucky dog you are, Ryland, squiring the two most beautiful ladies in London."

Belle laughed musically and began to flirt with Stratton. But Lucinda could not like the young man's coming manners and, in truth, she was rather shocked at Belle's forward response. Neither she nor Will took much part in the conversation.

Will was staring glumly at the passing scene when he exclaimed, "There's Charles Grantham!" He gestured to where Charles stood glowering at them. "Belle, I must speak to Grantham. Bid you good morning, Stratton."

Miles Stratton sighed extravagantly. "You will take the sunshine with you, Miss Ryland."

"Oh, fie, Mr. Stratton! I am sure you will find other suns—and other ladies." Belle tossed her blond curls in a way Lucinda found odiously coy.

"Macaroni merchant!" snorted Will as he urged his horses on.

"Do you think so? But he is such a superb dancer," Belle answered provocatively.

They took up Sir Charles, whose frown had grown alarmingly. His temper was not improved by Belle's continuing encomium of Miles Stratton. He ground his teeth audibly and responded to any attempts at conversation with a terse snap. Lucinda was quite out of patience with both him and Belle when Will touched her arm and pointed with his whip. Bounding towards them was a high-sprung phaeton pulled by two magnificent bays.

"Castor and Pollux!" Lucinda cried. Mr. Devereux was driving, and she recognized his companion as Lady Chloris dePoer. *C and R,* she thought with a sudden drop in her spirits.

Richard halted beside then and introduced Lady Chloris, who behaved correctly, if without any great degree of warmth. She was truly beautiful, Lucinda admitted, but so pale, and surely such excessive reserve could not be pleasing? She started as she realized Mr. Devereux was speaking to her.

"I wondered, Miss Neville, if you were pleased with the appearance of your former charges?"

"How could I not be, sir? They look decidedly splendid."

"Straining for a run, though. There is too much traffic to spring them here. But I trust you will soon be able to reassure yourself completely as to their well-being." He touched his whip to them as Chloris bade the group goodbye in her colourless well-bred voice.

Lucinda watched them depart. *What can he see in her?* she wondered. She was indeed a veritable Ice Queen.

"Well, Cinda," Will said, after they had set down Belle and Charles, still apparently on the outs with each other, to meet Lady Grantham. "What do you think of London now?"

Lucinda wrinkled her forehead. "It's quite different from what I expected. So many people, so many things to do and to see. And the shopping! Will, I had no idea people could spend so much time shopping."

"I can't," said Will with a grin.

Lucinda looked at him. He was more carefully dressed than he would be in the country. But no one was ever going to take his coat for one of Beau Devereux's. As she watched him turn into Agincourt Circle, Lucinda felt again how very *dear* he was: solid, sensible, unchanging Will.

"And of course," she said impulsively, "our being, you know, engaged has made it all so much easier for me. I am glad that you're in London, too, Will."

Will flushed a little and shifted in his seat. "Dashed generous idea of yours, Cinda; just like you."

"Hush." Lucinda raised her hand. "You are my dearest friend, Will. I should always want to help you."

The reins seemed suddenly to require a great deal of Mr. Ryland's attention. Then, clearing his throat a couple of times, he said, "Where is the London Hospice, Lucinda?"

"It's in the Isle of Dogs. Mr. Bunthorpe thinks that is the most salubrious location."

"Well, he's a sound chap. I expect he's right."

"Yes, I feel it quite remiss in me that I haven't been to visit him yet. Cousin Ethelreda says we shall go, but there seems to be so little time. I think perhaps she does not really want me to go. It's not that she disagrees with the idea; it's just that she thinks we shouldn't be so involved personally."

"Told Miss Grantham about it," Will's speech became progressively more staccato. "She's all for it. Said she'd like to see for herself. Told her I'd ask you."

"But that is the solution, Will. You and Patience and I shall go. Then we shan't have to bother cousin Ethelreda. What an excellent notion!" And Lucinda squeezed his hand affectionately before she took her leave.

IN THE MEANTIME, Mr. Devereux had returned Chloris to her mamà and was now at home, changing for his afternoon engagements. He was speaking his thoughts aloud, as was his wont, to his long-time valet. This was a thin, pinch-faced individual, who spoke so seldom that he was known below stairs as "Dumb" Dowsett.

"There can be, of course," Richard was saying, "no objection to Lady Chloris as an appropriate choice. She has beauty, breeding and manner. Her fortune is respectable, though that does not signify. What more could a man ask for in a wife?''

Dowsett proffered a perfectly laundered linen shirt. True to form, his usual expression of comprehensive disapproval did not vary.

''You are quite right, Dowsett.'' Mr. Devereux held out his arms for the cuff studs. ''Clearly I have windmills in the head to expect anything else.'' He took up a cravat. ''My Aunt Melpond is correct. It is high time I set up my nursery.''

Impassively, Dowsett watched as, in his first try, Mr. Devereux achieved a perfect Mathematical. He began to assist his master into his coat.

''You relieve my mind, Dowsett. I believe I must be suffering from the usual pangs of a bachelor contemplating matrimony. How lowering to realize that I am not free from such commonplace emotions.''

Dowsett smoothed the coat over his master's wide shoulders. With a final flick at his cravat, Mr. Devereux took himself off to meet Sir Charles at a modish coffee house.

His friend had arrived before him and as Devereux approached, he suddenly stopped and clutched at a chair back. ''Charles,'' he said, shutting his eyes. ''Charles, my dear fellow, is that—can it be—a *yellow* waistcoat?''

''Don't you like it, Dev?''

''No, Charles, I do not. I cannot claim any desire to dazzle the eyes of anyone unfortunate enough to glance my way.''

''It ain't that bright.''

"Do you think not?" Devereux asked solicitously. "And have you had this trouble with your eyes for a long time?"

Charles grinned. "All right, Dev, all right. Sit over there, where you're not looking straight at me." He beckoned the waiter and then changed the subject. "Wasn't that Chloris you were driving with this morning?"

"Yes, but I did not see you."

"Er, no." Sir Charles looked a little sheepish. "I was waiting for someone."

Richard raised one straight dark eyebrow. "I wonder if Ryland was driving his beautiful sister this morning?"

"Well, as a matter of fact, he was." Charles coloured at his friend's ironic expression. "And Miss Neville, of course. You know, Dev, I can't help thinking you're wrong about her. She isn't a man-eater at all. In truth, I'd say she was in a fair way to setting her cap at Ryland himself."

"Cupid has certainly been busy recently."

"Speaking of which, did you see Ivor at the Hoxboroughs'? He came late but as soon as he saw Mrs. Cleeson, he made a bee-line for her. I never saw Ivor so interested in the petticoat line before."

"I collect they are old acquaintances."

Sir Charles smiled wickedly. "Perhaps Ivor will surprise us all. Perhaps he will take a leg-shackle at last and save you from the Ice Queen."

Richard drained his coffee cup. "I wish I could convince you that I am looking for a wife, not a love match. Lady Chloris possesses all the necessary qualities for such a marital role.''

''Yes, yes, a veritable paragon.'' Sir Charles rose. ''Let us get on to Manton's then, Dev, or we shall have to wait for a gallery. Let us shoot and forget all about women.''

Devereux followed his friend out of the coffee house and firmly suppressed a rebellious memory of tiny gold stars twinkling in burnished curls.

CHAPTER SIX

LUCINDA'S DAYS grew ever more occupied. The Season was now in full swing. There were afternoon calls, morning calls, balls, assemblies, rout parties, theatre parties, breakfast parties, museum visits, concerts, diversions of all imaginable sorts.

She had eaten a cold supper in the Chinese Pavilion at Vauxhall; she had blushed at Mrs. Salmon's Waxworks, where the amorous shepherds and shepherdesses sported; she had been somewhat bored by the Elgin Marbles; she had marvelled at the Panorama's displays of Niagara Falls and of Pompeii and she had been truly amazed at the Appollonicon where "mechanical powers" performed daily.

"But what I have not seen," she said one afternoon as they walked in Rotten Row, "is the animals."

"Animals?" Will had been chatting with Patience and looked up at these words.

"I have heard there are tigers and monkeys and even an elephant."

They had walked almost as far as Stanhope Gate. Around the North Lodge a throng of beaux and ladies was milling. A tall figure detached himself and came to meet them.

"Good morning, Miss Neville, Miss Ryland. Your servant, Ryland."

"Good morning, sir." Belle smiled coquettishly at him. "Have you seen the elephant, Mr. Devereux?"

Mr. Devereux blinked. "Elephant? Ah, you must mean Chunee!"

"Is that his name?" Lucinda asked, laughing. "It sounds so outlandish."

"I hear there are many curiosities of the natural world to be seen in the Exeter 'Change," Patience said in her soft voice.

"Yes." Devereux nodded. "In Mr. Cross's Royal Menagerie. But Chunee is the most famous. Even Lord Byron visited him, you know."

"I did not know that. Then we must certainly go."

"I wonder we did not think of it before," Belle enthusiastically agreed.

Mr. Devereux cocked an eyebrow at Will. "Well, Ryland? We may take a hint, may we not? We are at your service, ladies. We shall conduct you to Chunee whenever you wish."

Lucinda looked at him in surprise. It seemed unlikely that visiting an elephant was Beau Devereux's idea of a stimulating afternoon. But he seemed quite serious and she joined her voice to the others' expression of thanks and pleasure.

BUT SUCH WERE THE DEMANDS of the social calendar that it was nearly a week later when the outing was finally arranged. In the meantime, Sir Charles had heard of the expedition and added himself to the party. Patience had, however, thought it over and decided that she did not care to view such ferocious animals.

"For you know," she said with a shudder, "that horses in the street have bolted when they heard the roars from the Menagerie."

"But what will you do?" Lucinda asked as they gathered in the Granthams' front salon.

"Will has offered to escort me to an exhibition of needlepoint pictures in Leicester Square, that is, if you do not mind, Lucinda?"

"Of course I do not mind. But," Lucinda added, turning wondering eyes on Will, "do you mean you would rather look at pictures than at an elephant?"

Will tugged at his cravat. Devereux closed his eyes at the havoc this wreaked on its arrangement. "Don't mind," Will muttered. "Saw the animals at the Tower already, you know, so it ain't the same thing."

"That's all right, then," Belle said happily. "So you may be on your way to Leicester Square and we shall make for the Strand."

Lucinda had, of course, heard of the Exeter 'Change and its number of small select shops, offering millinery, hosiery, books and any number of luxurious trifles. She knew also that it was a site much favoured for assignations, though that, naturally, was of little interest to her.

They turned into the Strand and stopped opposite the Savoy. Lucinda looked eagerly across the street to the sign of Mr. Edward Cross, Dealer in Foreign Birds and Beasts. Below the sign were a number of painted panels illustrating Mr. Cross's wares. In the middle was an imposing representation of an elephant.

"Do let's hurry," Lucinda urged.

Mr. Devereux looked down at her sparkling brown eyes and laughed. "Come along then, Miss Neville. It's upstairs here."

Once the party was inside the Menagerie, Lucinda's eyes widened. There were cages everywhere and the noise was overwhelming. But Richard took her elbow and guided her to one side.

"Here is the famous Chunee," he said, gesturing, but keeping his eyes on her face.

Involuntarily, Lucinda stepped closer to him. "I had not imagined him to be so... so gigantic."

"Five tons, I apprehend."

Lucinda looked somewhat nervously at the huge reinforced bars and thick ropes of the cage. "He must be enormously strong."

"But he is said to conduct himself most quietly." Sir Charles had joined them. Despite his comment, however, he made sure he stood protectively close to Miss Ryland.

"Lord Byron thought him so well behaved that he wished him for his butler," Dev told them.

As if overhearing his remark, Chunee lifted up his trunk and trumpeted stentoriously. Both Belle and Lucinda clapped their hands to their ears.

"Heavens," gasped Miss Neville when relative quiet was at last restored. "I certainly wouldn't have a butler who did that." She took a last look at the great grey beast, then turned to the other cages. There were furry grey monkeys whose antics made them all laugh and a cage full of parrots whose splendid plumage contrasted strangely with their raucous cries.

Mr. Devereux had also told them that Lord Byron had enjoyed watching the tigers being fed. But when Lucinda and Belle saw the great buckets of bloody meat being carried in, they both voted rather quickly to leave at once.

Downstairs, they recovered their equilibrium and were more than willing to stroll through the long enclosed gallery, lined on both sides with small stalls. The arcade was crowded and they met many acquaintances.

Mr. Devereux and Sir Charles had stopped to look at a volume of Hogarth's engravings and Belle had called to Lucinda to see a *diamanté* comb in the neighbouring stalls. As Belle debated the merits of the hair ornament, a poster caught Lucinda's eye.

She read it with widening eyes. "Oh, Mr. Devereux, do look," she said urgently.

He read it with a slight twitch at the corner of his mobile mouth. "No, Miss Neville," he said with a twinkle in his grey eyes. "Chunee I can accept. But when it cames to Toby, the Sapient Pig, I cry craven."

"But do look, sir. It says he will spell and read and tell the time."

"And play cards." Belle came and peered over Lucinda's shoulder.

"No! Really? Let me see." Sir Charles read, too. "By Jove, I've played cards with donkeys before, but never with a swine."

They all laughed, but suddenly Devereux looked up and stopped. Following his gaze, Lucinda saw Lady Chloris dePoer staring wide-eyed at them.

"Oh!" Lady Chloris was deeply flushed and her bosom heaved as she gazed at them.

Devereux bowed and took her hand. "Chloris! How pleasant, I had not thought to see you here."

It was too crowded for more than two people to walk together, so Lucinda dropped behind. Sir Charles had reattached himself to Belle, so she had naturally supposed Chloris would take Mr. Devereux's arm. But to her surprise, she found herself beside Chloris. In front of them, Belle and Sir Charles were flirting again, and ahead of them, Mr. Devereux sauntered nonchalantly.

She stole a sideways glance at Chloris. Today her ladyship wore ice-blue muslin. It flattered her pale beauty but, Lucinda considered, it added credibility to her nickname. However, one had to admit that today Chloris had a little more colour. She was somewhat breathless, as if she had been running.

Chloris, it seemed, was interested in her, too, for suddenly their eyes met and each laughed a little self-consciously.

"You and Mr. Devereux are great friends, are you not?" Chloris asked in an artificially casual tone.

But Lucinda was not deceived. She heard the note of urgency in the other girl's voice. Surely Lady Chloris could not be jealous of her?

"Oh, no, Lady Chloris." She made her voice sound coolly indifferent. "I should not say so, not at all."

"I only asked because I have seen him dance with you on a number of occasions and I believe that you share a common interest in some horses?"

"Mr. Devereux has been obliging enough to honour me with a dance," Lucinda said, "and he has acquired some horses which were bred in my father's stables. He has been kind enough to assure us of their safety." Then, in a rush, she went on, "It is because he is so obliging that he is with us today, for Mr. Ryland was to accompany us, but he was called away."

It wasn't precisely a lie, she told herself, and anyway, she had to allay Chloris's suspicious at all costs. In this it seemed she was successful, for Chloris sighed and was silent for a moment. Then she turned to the stall they were passing.

"Look, Miss Neville. Is this not the most cunningly devised thing? It looks just like a rose, but it is made entirely of tulle."

Lucinda responded suitably, and with such unexceptionable small talk they came to the Strand entrance.

Chloris gestured to her maid who was following. "We have left the carriage by Simpson's there. I am afraid I must hurry off for I am to meet my mama." She bade them farewell and Mr. Devereux conducted her to the waiting carriage.

As though absently, Lucinda shifted her position on the pavement so that she might watch him hand Chloris into the vehicle. They did not look lover-like, she considered. But then, of course, such well-bred persons would never display their private feelings in public.

With a guilty start, she thought again of the love-token. She must do something with it. But if Chloris already suspected her of developing a tendre for Mr. Devereux, she would have to be even more careful in restoring it. She sighed and looked askance at her two companions.

"La, sir!" Belle slapped Sir Charles playfully on the wrist. "How can you say such things?"

Sir Charles struck a dashing pose. "My dear Miss Ryland, you have no idea of how I am willing to dare, especially for so tempting a prize."

"Come, Charles." Mr. Devereux had returned and now tapped his friend on the shoulder. "That is indeed a striking attitude, but take my advice, do not waste it on the Strand. Save it for Almack's or the next ball, where it will have the audience it deserves."

Sir Charles laughed good-naturedly, and he and Belle got into their own carriage. Mr. Devereux

handed Lucinda up and then seated himself opposite her.

The others were in merry pin, but Lucinda felt that
all her pleasure in the event had evaporated. Indeed,
she refused an invitation to Gunther's and requested
Mr. Devereux to drive her back to Agincourt Circle.

To Mrs. Cleeson's enquiry as to how the afternoon had gone, she responded only that the noise
had given her a headache. She immediately retired to
her room till it was time for the evening's events.

WHEN LUCINDA CAME DOWNSTAIRS the next morning, she found Mrs. Cleeson standing in the hall with
a long list in her hand.

"Oh, dear, oh, dear," her cousin was muttering.
"Did I say the rose brocade or the violet damask?
Because, you know, if I said the damask, then I must
change the cushions' colour, for of course the yellow will not suit the damask."

"Whatever is the matter, cousin Ethelreda?"

"Oh! Good morning, Lucinda. I have just sent a
footman off to Chippendale's and I must send another down to the draper's and I cannot remember
which curtains I ordered for the front salon."

Lucinda glanced at the list, but it was so criss-
crossed with additions and scratchings-out that she
could make little of it. "Well, cousin," she said reasonably, "why don't you wait till the footman comes
back and you can ask him? Then you may send to the
draper's in complete surety."

"I suppose I had best do so. But I must also see to the wallpaper for the breakfast parlour. Now where is my list for that?"

"After breakfast," Lucinda urged, and steered her cousin down the hall.

Breakfast, however, did not soothe Mrs. Cleeson's anxieties. She ate distractedly, peering and muttering at her lists. At length, she put them down.

"Lucinda, I have quite made up my mind. Unless you should dislike it excessively, I shall cancel our morning engagements. We cannot begin to entertain until the house is completely in order, and the time for your ball grows closer. I believe I must go to Gedge's myself and see about the tablecloths and the other linens and then of course there are the curtains for the bedrooms and..."

Laughing, Lucinda held up her hand. "Very well, very well, cousin Ethelreda. It is most kind in you to have undertaken such a prodigious task. Papa must be overwhelmed when he sees the transformation. By all means take the time you require."

"You have no objection to not meeting our engagements?"

"Not at all, but I should be glad to help you in your errands."

"Thank you, dearest; not for me, but for yourself perhaps."

"How so, cousin?"

"I think you might take Albert and do some shopping. You could do with some more silk stockings. I would like to see a new bonnet for the azure muslin. Then you need gloves, and I have never been happy with the green boots and the sprig-muslin, so you might..."

"Enough, enough, cousin! I shall need more than one afternoon for so many commissions. If you think it fitting, I shall go back to the Exeter 'Change, for I was much taken with the wares there."

"The very thing, my dear. You are sure to find what you want there. But—" she wagged a finger "—be careful what you buy: no Cranbourne Alley articles!"

Lucinda laughed again and promised. It was with a gratifying sense of freedom and sophistication that she set out with her footman.

It was delightful to wander again by the various stalls, picking up a lacy shawl here, a pair of pearl combs there, adding a blue-dyed ostrich plume now, then a painted Chinese fan. Soon Albert was struggling to hold the proliferating parcels.

Lucinda paused by a tray of ribbons. She was thoughtfully fingering a length of cherry grosgrain when a soft drawl behind her made her jump. She whirled round to find Mr. Devereux regarding her with a rather quizzical expression.

"No, Miss Neville." He shook his head at her. "No."

"No?" Lucinda looked down at the ribbon in her hand. "Do you mean you do not care for this shade?"

"Not with that hair."

Lucinda chuckled huskily. "You needn't shudder. I wasn't really going to buy it. It's just," she went on, looking a trifle wistful, "I look so very insipid in the pale colours young ladies are supposed to wear."

"Believe me, Miss Neville, no one could possibly describe you as insipid."

Lucinda blushed and looked away. Then a thought struck her and the great brown eyes flew to his face. "Oh, sir, I did not mean, that is, I was not . . ."

"Angling for compliments, do you mean? Again, Miss Neville, no one who knew you could suppose for a minute that you were."

Lucinda smiled uncertainly. Was he quizzing her? Or even, unlikely as it seemed, flirting with her?

Devereux watched the emotions play across her face with amusement. Then, telling himself sternly that he must not take undue advantage of her inexperience, he said kindly, "Are you wondering what brings me back to the 'Change so soon after our visit?"

"Well, er, yes." Lucinda had been so surprised to see him at all that she had not thought to question his appearance.

"I saw your carriage outside and I took the opportunity to apologize."

"Apologize, sir? I do not understand."

Mr. Devereux was not sure he himself understood the impulse that had made him stop at the sight of the Neville carriage and had brought him into an establishment he would normally have passed in total indifference. However, he offered an explanation as much to himself as to Lucinda.

"I have not forgotten my promise to show you Castor and Pollux, but we have both been much occupied. I have thought of that promise and of you often, Miss Neville."

Lucinda blushed again at the thought she had been in Beau Devereux's thoughts. Somehow, it made her feel happy but at the same time a little nervous.

"Is Mrs. Cleeson with you?"

"She's much occupied this afternoon. Albert, my footman, is with me."

Devereux looked at that long-suffering man. "Let me make it up to you for my neglect, Miss Neville. Send Albert home with the packages. He may inform Mrs. Cleeson I have taken you for a drive and will bring you home later." He saw the hesitation and also the eagerness in Lucinda's eyes. "It is quite proper, Miss Neville. My tiger will be present and we shall be in an open vehicle."

"I should like to," said Lucinda, telling herself that it was obviously her duty to see how Castor and Pollux did.

"Then come," said Mr. Devereux.

And Lucinda did. She sent the grateful Albert and her purchases home and followed Mr. Devereux through the crowded gallery. At one stall, he stopped so suddenly that she almost bumped into him.

He held out an arm to steady her. "Miss Neville, do I understand you to be tired of the pale colours young ladies are obliged to wear?"

"I don't feel that they quite suit," Lucinda confessed rather hesitantly, uncertain whether this was the sort of topic one discussed with gentlemen.

"I've told you what I think of that. But you are wanting something out of the ordinary, are you?"

"Yes, very much."

"Then, look here."

"Gold lace," Lucinda breathed. "Gold Brussels lace—but, do you think it quite the thing, sir?"

Devereux's eyebrows rose slightly. "I would not suggest it otherwise." Then his tone softened. "It will certainly be quite the thing with your hair." *And with those extraordinary eyes,* he added to himself.

Lucinda touched the cobwebby fabric. "It is so fragile."

Mr. Devereux's next remark surprised even himself. "And you must be sure to wear those gold stars in your hair."

Lucinda smiled radiantly at him. "Did you like them, sir? They were my mother's, you know, but cousin Ethelreda thought they might perhaps be somewhat démodé."

"Certainly not," said Beau Devereux.

So Lucinda bought the requisite amount of gold lace and soon afterwards found herself bowling northwards in Mr. Devereux's perfectly sprung vehicle.

CHAPTER SEVEN

"HOW SPLENDIDLY they run," said Lucinda, as the bays strode effortlessly out along the Highgate Road. "They are in plump currant indeed."

"We are making for Hampstead Heath," Mr. Devereux told her. "There they, as well as I, shall be able to show you our paces."

He was as good as his word, and Lucinda enjoyed herself enormously. The wind blew her bonnet backwards and she laughed as her curls streamed behind her. Most of all, Mr. Devereux's light but masterful control of the reins impressed her mightily.

They did not speak much, but rather enjoyed the fresh air, the swift horses and, though each had different reasons for not admitting it, each other's company.

"Come," said Richard at last, "I must get you home. Your cousin will be worried if you do not appear soon and you will be late for your afternoon tea."

"I suppose so." Reluctantly, Lucinda straightened her bonnet. "But it is such a relief to know Castor and Pollux are so well taken care of."

She had quite revised her opinion of Mr. Devereux. He was no longer a proud, overbearing care-for-nought. He was charming, thoughtful, the most obliging of companions. Not once did the memory of Lady Chloris dePoer or a certain piece of jewellery cloud her mind.

Nothing on the homeward journey challenged Lucinda's new conviction. She was in perfect charity with him as they turned into the crowded streets about the Kentish Town market.

Suddenly a shout rang out. A small boy darted out between the fruit and vegetable carts. Mr. Devereux cursed once and pulled on the ribbons. Castor neighed shrilly, reared, and as he came down, one flailing hoof caught the boy on the side of his head. The small figure fell and lay still.

Mr. Devereux cursed again and, tossing the reins to his tiger, leapt down. He was scarcely quicker than Lucinda, however. She reached the boy before he did and, heedless of the dust, knelt beside the child.

"Miss Neville," began Richard, "do you not think that you would be advised to retire to..."

Lucinda loosened the boy's grubby jerkin and then took up one small, limp hand. She did not look up as she replied, "Of course not. How should I be when I am needed here?" She laid the little hand back on the boy's chest. "I don't believe he has been seriously hurt, but one cannot be too careful with injuries to the head."

Mr. Devereux watched her with an unreadable expression in his grey eyes. Then he said, "What do you wish done, Miss Neville?"

Lucinda looked anxiously at the boy, then at the crowd of onlookers. "Ordinarily, I should not care to move him, but we can scarcely let him lie in the middle of the thoroughfare."

"Where shall we take him, then?" If Mr. Devereux thought it odd that he should leave the resolution of this affair to a "schoolroom chit," he gave no sign.

"To the Isle of Dogs," Lucinda said decisively. "I know the warden of the hospice there."

"Of course! I should have thought of that myself."

Lucinda found this response odd, but before she could speak, Richard continued, "Return to the phaeton, Miss Neville. I shall carry the child up to you. It will be best if you hold him as we drive."

"But of course I shall, the poor mite," Lucinda said as she climbed back into her seat.

Mr. Devereux spoke briefly to certain members of the crowd and some coins changed hands. Then he carefully lifted the small figure and placed him on Lucinda's lap.

He noted that Miss Neville paid no more attention to the stains from the boy's boots than she had to those from the dust of the road. Rather to Lucinda's surprise, Mr. Devereux asked for no directions. Manoeuvring skilfully through the heavy traffic, he brought them south to the river and at last to the wide black gates of the hospice.

It was a low, sprawling whitewashed building, set amid green fields inclining down to the river. A blue-clad attendant met them and, quickly grasping the situation, summoned two more blue-clad helpers, who bore the boy away on a litter. Lucinda and Devereux were shown into a small office where the warden joined them. A kindly man with thick grey hair, Mr. Bunthorpe was clearly delighted to see Lucinda.

"Miss Neville, we heard that you were in London and knew that it could not be long before you visited us."

"I wish it had been sooner," Lucinda said. "But may I present..."

"Bless you, Miss Neville, don't you know? There is no need to introduce Mr. Devereux to us. He's our new governor."

"You!" Lucinda gaped at him. "You! I did not know you were interested in such things."

Mr. Devereux's smile went slightly awry. "How should you, Miss Neville? I did not know you shared so fully in your father's concerns."

"Yes, indeed." Mr. Bunthorpe beamed. "Miss Neville is one of our strongest supporters. She has helped us in so many ways. What we should have done without her in our early days I dare not think."

"My own association is not so longstanding," Mr. Devereux told her. "Nor can I hope to be so invaluable. Your father recruited me only recently, and he is to inform me more fully of my duties when he comes up to Town. It seems to me to be a most necessary work."

"Necessary, indeed," Mr. Bunthorpe echoed, nodding vigorously. "How can the poor improve their circumstances, unless they first improve their health?" He twinkled reprovingly. "But you must not be too modest, Mr. Devereux, we have heard of your ground-breaking work in other areas."

Lucinda looked from one to the other in surprise. Devereux looked as nearly embarrassed as she'd ever seen him. "What other..."

Dev rose hastily. "I am sure Miss Neville would like to see your establishment here," he said to the warden, "but we are already long overdue and must not agitate Mrs. Cleeson further."

"And you will be sure to let us know how the poor little boy does?" Lucinda said anxiously.

"Dear me!" Mr. Bunthorpe looked comically dismayed. "I have a head like a sieve. He was coming round when I left. The doctor feels that he will sustain no lasting hurt, but we shall keep him here for a few days just to make sure. I understand that you have already sent word to the parents. We shall be in touch with them also."

"Let me know before you send him back to them," said Mr. Devereux. "He does not look as though his family's circumstances are prosperous. We must see what can be done for them."

They took leave of Mr. Bunthorpe and returned to the phaeton. Lucinda waited until they were moving again, then she said firmly, "Pray, sir, what is the other work that Mr. Bunthorpe says you do?"

"Shall I puff off my poor efforts to you, Miss Neville? They are a mere nothing compared to the achievements of you and your father."

"My papa says that any effort is praiseworthy," said Lucinda seriously. "And I should so very much like to know."

Mr. Devereux looked at her and his clear gaze softened. "Your father is far more perceptive than my aunt," he said. "I have tried to alleviate a little, a very little, the plight of the widows and orphans in the slums around the docks here."

Lucinda's eyes shone. "Oh, sir," she cried, "I thought you were just a heartless Town beau. I have misjudged you terribly."

There was a light in Mr. Devereux's eyes that had not been there before. "I think you are not the only one who has made a misjudgement, Miss Neville."

"Please, sir, will you not tell me all about your work?"

"I will, Miss Neville, I promise you. But now I wish you will tell me how you and your father conceived the idea of the hospices."

The news that Mr. Devereux was interested in the work that was so dear to her completed the evolution of Lucinda's feelings. She felt she had been guilty of assuming much too quickly that he could have no interests beyond Town amusements. Now she talked freely.

"It began with an accident. One of our farm workers injured himself with a scythe: a very bad cut, almost severing his arm. Papa saw he was not getting better; he was not getting the proper care. I went to see him myself and the arm was dreadfully infected. His wound was not being properly cleaned and he was not being fed the proper food, either. And he was not the only one in such a situation."

Lucinda went on to explain how they had set up the Nether Wilden Hospice for the Sick and Injured and how, after one patient had spoken of the conditions of his brother in London, they had established the second hospice in the Isle of Dogs.

Mr. Devereux asked an occasional question, but mostly he was content to listen, to watch her constantly changing face and to think. Her gown was creased and stained, her bonnet askew. A mass of thick, glossy curls had escaped confinement and cascaded down one cheek. There was a tiny smudge on the end of her nose.

Catching one of his intent glances, Lucinda suddenly became aware of her disheveled state. She put up a hand to push back the errant locks.

"No." Mr. Devereux raised his own hand as though to stop her. "Pray do not. They look charmingly."

All at once, Lucinda felt shy. She turned her eyes towards the horses. As she sensed his continuing gaze, her constraint grew, her flow of conversation dried up and she began to wish for home.

At length they drew up in Agincourt Circle. Mr. Devereux came round to help Lucinda down. As he stretched his arms up to her, Lucinda's eyes met his and a spark seemed to fly between them.

His arms went round her waist. He lifted her, not to the ground, but towards him. Lucinda felt the strength in his arms, saw his lips come closer, was burnt by that fiery stare. She raised her face, felt the world swim about her, then . . .

Into her mind there flashed the memory of a pretty little trinket, citrines and diamonds, C and R interlinked. "No," she cried, "no, no!"

For a long moment he held her, suspended, before him. Then, slowly, he lowered her to the ground, his arms falling away to his sides. Lucinda ducked her head, muttered a few incoherent words and fled up the steps.

Mr. Devereux stared after her. Then, turning swiftly, he leapt into the phaeton. With a savage tug on the reins that made his tiger cry out in protest, he urged the bays into a gallop.

And that, he told himself, *is that. A fine display from a man who is supposed to know women.*

He did not stop at Agincourt Crescent. Instead he made straight for St. James's and the clubs. There he spent the night becoming efficiently and thoroughly drunk.

CHAPTER EIGHT

LUCINDA DID NOT SEE Mr. Devereux for the next few days. That, she told herself, was a piece of great good fortune. It was, naturally, only a desire to avoid an uncomfortable scene that made her scan the crowds for his tall languid figure. And of course it was only relief she felt when she failed to see him.

Fortunately, her cousin was much too preoccupied to take much notice of Lucinda's moods. Mrs. Cleeson was in the final stages of refurbishing the house. A steady stream of tradesmen had visited Agincourt Circle. Lucinda had been shown endless samples of paint, cloth and wallpapers and miniatures of furniture.

Matters at Gedge's and Chippendale's and a dozen other establishments had all been settled. Mrs. Cleeson had driven to Mr. Wedgewood's extensive showroom in Grosvenor Square and ordered new china.

That very morning, the last vase and mirror had been delivered. Now Lucinda stood in the window of the newly resplendent front salon. She was fidgeting with the purple tassels on the new violet draperies.

Behind her, seated beside Ivor Devereux on the equally new red morocco sofa, Mrs. Cleeson triumphantly drew a large X through her list and tucked it away in her reticule.

"Now at last I may begin a new list, one that has nothing whatever to do with refurbishing."

"And dare I hope that you will place the matter of which we spoke near the top of any such list?" Ivor asked softly.

"Oh, hush, Ivor." Mrs. Cleeson cast a quick glance at Lucinda. "Shall we see you at the Vernissage this afternoon?" she asked, raising her voice in exaggerated cheerfulness.

"What? At the Royal Academy? No, my dear. Not my choice at all. You keen on pictures, then?" This last was addressed to Lucinda.

She turned with a start. "I have never attended such an event, Mr. Devereux."

"Ah, well, best to go and see for yourself, then." Ivor stood. "I hope you enjoy the crush."

Mrs. Cleeson rose as well and escorted him to the door. Her colour was high when she returned, but Lucinda was still staring out at the empty street.

"Mercy, child!" Ethelreda shrieked. "Don't twist the tassel off before it's been in the house a week."

"Sorry, cousin." Lucinda dropped the silk bundle but remained standing in the same listless way.

Mrs. Cleeson looked narrowly at her. "Are you sure you're feeling quite the thing, Lucinda?"

"Yes, cousin."

Mrs. Cleeson frowned. "You haven't quarrelled with Will, have you?"

"Will? Of course not. He's coming to the Royal Academy with us."

"In that case..." Cousin Ethelreda's voice trailed off. If it wasn't a lovers' quarrel that was ailing the girl, what could it be? Lucinda had been uncharacteristically on edge these past few days.

Later that afternoon, however, Mrs. Cleeson had to admit that her charge had apparently recovered from the mopes. She seemed in merry pin as they met Belle, Patience, Sir Charles and Lady Grantham.

In fact, Lucinda had decided she was making too much of the scene with Mr. Devereux. He was a Town beau, after all, and she, she had to admit, was a green girl. She had talked to him with too much familiarity and she had always heard that gentlemen were prone to misinterpret such forwardness. She was refining too much upon it.

So Lucinda laughed and chatted as animatedly as Belle as they drove up to the door of Somerset House. There were many other vehicles crowding the street and a throng of elegantly dressed persons milling about on the pavement.

Lucinda saw clearly what Ivor had meant about the crowd. But once they were inside the famous Great Room, the press abated not one whit.

The girls stared wide-eyed about them. *Vernissage,* Lucinda knew, meant *varnishing.* She had half expected to see artists and easels, but all the works were elaborately framed and hung.

"What a number of pictures!" Patience exclaimed.

"There are generally over five hundred works on view," Lady Grantham told them.

"They are hung all the way up the walls." Lucinda craned her neck towards the domed ceiling. "I can scarcely make out what the higher ones are about."

"And there are some almost at floor level." Belle gestured. "One would have practically to lie down to see them."

"I recall my father telling me that Mr. Gainsborough declared that if the Committee hung his picture up there 'in the sky,' he would never send another to the Academy," Sir Charles said with a chuckle.

"And did they?" Lucinda asked.

"They did and he didn't."

"I don't wonder at it," she said. "Why, I cannot tell what some of them may represent at all."

"I can scarcely see any of them," Patience said, looking about. "There are so many people here."

"We must get a catalogue," Sir Charles decided. "That will tell us what we are seeing—or not seeing."

"A good idea, Charles," his mother said with a nod. She turned to Mrs. Cleeson. "I see a bench over there, Ethelreda. Let us sit there while the young people walk about."

Mrs. Cleeson consented and the two chaperons watched their charges with indulgent smiles.

"How charmingly Lucinda looks today," Lady Grantham remarked.

"And Belle is always beautiful," Mrs. Cleeson said with equal magnanimity. "I am so glad, too, to see Patience in her best looks."

Lady Grantham smiled, then sighed. "I believe that Charles has developed a tendre for my god-daughter."

"And you do not approve?"

Lady Grantham shrugged. "She is a pretty child, somewhat wild, but when one considers..." The eyes of the two chaperons met.

"Quite so." Ethelreda nodded. "Lady Ryland's influence is not the ideal one for a young girl. But, Amelia, would you welcome Belle as a daughter-in-law?"

"If that is what Charles wants, I shall not stand in his way. Though I should, I own, prefer him to choose a less...well, a less volatile girl."

"But..." Mrs. Cleeson spoke rather hesitantly. "I do not mean to suggest that Charles himself is vola-tile, but he does seem to enjoy..." She stopped.

"Enjoy play-acting?" His mother nodded re-signedly. "He has, I'm afraid, a dramatic streak."

"Then, you know, he might perhaps find a more placid girl actually boring."

"You may be right, Ethelreda. But if that is the case, I wish Belle will not so deliberately provoke him by flirting with Miles Stratton."

"Amelia! Surely she cannot be serious about that!"

"Oh, I think not." Lady Grantham sighed for a third time. "And there is Patience."

"I cannot think Patience could cause you any anxiety."

"Not really, I suppose. But I wish she would show some sign of finding someone interesting. She is polite to them all and says that they are agreeable, but," said Lady Grantham astringently, "unless I much miss my guess, she would not notice if any of them fell off the Earth and were never seen again."

"Perhaps she has simply not yet met anyone who captures her fancy."

"Well, of course I should not coerce her into a union she found distasteful, but I do wish she would show a little more *enthusiasm*."

"When she finds the right gentleman," Mrs. Cleeson said soothingly, "I've no doubt she shall."

Patience's mother snorted but left the topic. "You, Ethelreda, are fortunate in your charge. Lucinda seems to have fixed her interest on young Ryland. Even if the father's pockets are to let, I hear nothing but good about the boy and he, so I hear, inherits the grandfather's fortune."

"Ye-e-es. Will is a delightful young man."

"But you sound dubious, Ethelreda."

"Not about Will's character. But he and Lucinda have known each other all their lives, and I have never before suspected they cherished a tendre for each other at all."

"Such a change in feelings is not unknown as young people grow up."

"True." Mrs. Cleeson shook her head. "But I have sometimes thought . . . in fact, at times, I have been almost convinced that . . ."

But the source of Mrs. Cleeson's conviction was never to be revealed. Two other ladies appeared and greeted them effusively. Lady Grantham and Ethelreda made room for them on the bench and no more private matters were discussed.

Meanwhile, catalogues in hand, the younger members of the party squeezed past the crowds and tried to look at the pictures. Belle and Sir Charles fell behind, giggling over some private joke of their own.

Patience was reading from the catalogue while Will listened in apparent rapture. On the whole, Lucinda thought, the crowd was more intriguing than the pictures, and certainly easier to study.

She had seen many members of the haut ton, all conversing vivaciously with one another, oblivious to the art surrounding them. As she looked over the crowd, she started a little, for not far from her, staring expressionlessly at a full-length portrait of the Prince Regent, was Lady Chloris dePoer.

The crowd parted for a moment; Chloris looked up and saw Lucinda. She smiled politely and nodded.

To her annoyance, Lucinda flushed. She began to incline her own head, but the crowd had closed between them again. *Thank heavens,* Lucinda thought, Mr. Devereux was nowhere near them. But there was still that brooch, and she had to find a way of returning it!

She looked at Will and Patience. Their heads were close together, bent over the catalogue. She glanced at the picture before them—*Fox's Litter at Play*—and concluded that it scarcely warranted such study. First the needlepoint exhibition, and now this. She had never known Will had such a passion for art.

She risked a glance over the crowd again. She did not see Chloris again, but she did spy Lady Hoxborough, wearing one of her amazing turbans, this one set with a huge, balefully twinkling emerald. Her ladyship was talking, but Lucinda could not see to whom. The unfortunate victim was evidently not getting much of a chance to contribute to the conversation, for Lady Hoxborough's lips never stopped.

Curiously, Lucinda stepped to one side and peered round a couple of loudly arguing gentlemen. She went hot and then cold. For a moment, she felt sheer panic and looked wildly about for an escape.

The person Lady Hoxborough was addressing was Beau Devereux. He leant one hand against the wall, his head was courteously inclined and his expression was one of total absorption.

He was not looking her way, but Lucinda immediately stepped back behind the two gentlemen. He must not see her!

Will and Patience were now both admiring a painting of London Bridge, her dark head close to his fair one. Hurriedly, Lucinda made some excuse to them and threaded her way back to the bench.

She found Mrs. Cleeson and Lady Grantham surrounded by a number of friends who welcomed her into their conversation. However, Lucinda positioned herself where she could see the exit and gave only half an ear to their chatter.

She saw Lady Hoxborough make a stately departure, but Mr. Devereux did not leave the Great Room. She could not doubt that as soon as he had been released by Lady Hoxborough, he had made directly for Prinny's portrait and Lady Chloris.

CHAPTER NINE

IF COUSIN ETHELREDA had thought Lucinda improved at Somerset House, next morning she reverted to her previous misgivings. As was becoming usual, Ivor Devereux had called as early as a morning visit might reasonably be paid. He and Mrs. Cleeson broke off their tête-à-tête when Lucinda entered the front salon.

But Lucinda did not sit down and join in their conversation. Instead, she flitted about, picking up a japanned box here, a pot-pourri dish there. She rearranged the roses in a bowl on the table, straightened three pillows on the confidante, picked up and down in turn each ornament on the mantelpiece until at last Mrs. Cleeson burst out.

"I declare, Lucinda, you are as mifty as a sick cat these days. I do hope you are not sickening for something."

"Wouldn't say the girl was mifty," put in Ivor. "A little pale, though. Goin' the pace probably. Needs some good country air. Take her out to Dorking, bring the roses back to those cheeks."

"Ivor, the very thing. What do you say, Lucinda? Are you tired of Town pleasures?"

Town had certainly seemed to lose a good deal of its appeal recently, so Lucinda was pleased by the idea of a country expedition. And, she thought wryly, she wouldn't be likely to run into Lady Chloris in the middle of Dorking Wood.

THUS, WHEN MR. RICHARD Devereux turned into Agincourt Circle early the next morning, his uncle's cheery voice hailed him.

"Hi, Ricky, over here!" Ivor was standing on the steps of the Granthams' travelling coach. Lady Grantham was inside and Mrs. Cleeson stood on the pathway, perusing the inevitable list.

Richard greeted the two elder ladies. "Well, Ivor," he said then, "you look poised for adventure."

"Off to Dorking, my boy. Luncheon alfresco. Care to join us? You'd be better off for a day out of Town."

"Yes, do come, Dev." Sir Charles had ridden up on a big grey.

"It will be so delightful to be in the country," Lady Grantham said, leaning out of the window. "For, you know, it is to be an excessively hot day today."

"It is a tempting prospect," Devereux agreed, but his eyes were on the open landau just in front, in which Lucinda, Belle and Patience made a cool and charming picture in their gauzy summer muslins. "But I am dressed neither for the country nor for riding."

"Go and change, my boy. You'll easily catch up with us or your stable ain't what it used to be."

Mr. Devereux regarded the landau. Belle smiled and waved; Patience nodded politely. Lucinda apparently did not see him, for she was gazing with deep interest at a small black-and-white dog which was investigating the gutter. Mr. Devereux smiled slightly.

"Thank you, your ladyship." He bowed to Lady Grantham. "I shall be honoured to join you."

Lucinda watched him leave with mixed feelings. Her heart had been unaccountably lightened when she saw him first, but when he looked towards the landau, she had been sure he meant to approach them and felt a sensation that was close to panic. Now she was conscious of strong disappointment.

"What happened to Mr. Devereux?" Belle demanded as Sir Charles rode up to them again. "Why didn't you ask him to join us?"

"He's going to," Charles replied, frowning at Belle's interest. "He's just gone to change."

"Mr. Devereux is always agreeable," said Patience soothingly. "I am sure we shall all be glad to have him join us. Aren't you, Lucinda?"

Miss Neville tried to speak casually, but her voice sounded strained, even to her own ears. "Of...of course."

In sudden concern Patience asked, "Are you nervous about the journey? I do not think you need be, for in general, you know, people are not sick in open carriages."

"No, no, I'm sure I shan't be. Look, my cousin has finally got into the coach. Now we shall be on our way."

"That's right," Will agreed as he cantered up, "we're off to Dorking!"

It was a bright, glorious morning and Belle and Patience were soon in high gig. They bantered playfully with Charles and Will. But Lucinda was mostly silent, and when Mr. Devereux galloped up on an enormous chestnut, she became entirely so.

Their destination was a pretty meadow, bordered by Dorking Wood on one side and a sparkling crystal brook on another. Soon Lady Grantham and Mrs. Cleeson, with Ivor Devereux in attendance, were installed in the shade of an ancient elm. Then the younger members of the party busied themselves in unpacking the picnic baskets.

Lucinda was uncomfortably aware of Richard Devereux. As she worked, she made quite sure that she was never beside him. At lunch, she positioned herself quickly between Belle and Mrs. Cleeson.

If Mr. Devereux noticed these elaborate manoeuvres, he kept the knowledge to himself and made no attempt to single Lucinda out. He addressed no more remarks to her than to the others and treated her with his usual impersonal courtesy.

Lucinda was not sure whether to be pleased or piqued by this treatment. However, she did relax a little. Once the repast was finished, however, all her apprehensions returned.

Lady Grantham and Mrs. Cleeson showed an inclination to drowse against the bole of their tree. Producing a fat cigar, Ivor removed himself to the far edge of the wood to smoke it.

Sir Charles invited Belle to walk in the woods, "To look for primroses," he suggested.

If Belle was aware that the time for primroses had long since passed, she made no sign. Instead she fluttered her lashes at her eager swain. "Why, yes," she said, "do let us explore this darling wood."

Mr. Devereux was still lounging with a glass of wine, but Lucinda decided to forestall any plans he might have. "Come, Will," she said brightly, standing up and holding out her hand. "I do so want to look at this delightful little brook."

"Eh?" Will gaped at her, then seeing her still waiting, he scrambled up. "The brook? Right!" He took her arm, and with a last look backwards, went with Lucinda.

Mr. Devereux turned to Patience. "Would you care to walk also, Miss Grantham?"

Patience withdrew her gaze from Will and Lucinda. "Why yes, sir. That would be the very thing."

He helped her up. "Which way do you prefer, then?"

Without raising her eyes, Patience said, "I think, you know, I should like to walk beside the stream. It is so pretty there."

"An admirable choice," said Mr. Devereux gravely. "Shall we go?" And they followed in Will and Lucinda's wake.

"What's all this about the stream?" the former was demanding. "I mean, it's just a stream. Dozens of 'em in Nether Wilden and I never heard you in alt about any of 'em before."

Instead of answering, Lucinda stole a glance behind her. She had seen Patience and Mr. Devereux rise; now they were clearly engaged in lively and amusing conversation. Will peered round too and grunted. They trudged on in gloomy silence.

Silence, however, did not mark the encounter between Belle and Sir Charles. After going a short way into the wood, they had spied a rather picturesque fallen log and had seated themselves upon it. Unfortunately, his evil angel prompted Sir Charles to reproach Belle for her friendship with Miles Stratton.

Miss Ryland sat up straighter. "What! Do you mean to criticize my behaviour, sir?"

Sir Charles began to retreat. "I didn't mean anything of the sort, Belle, don't—"

"And just what *did* you mean?"

"Dash it all, Belle, everyone knows about Stratton: you meet him everywhere, but he ain't good ton. You ask Dev if—"

Her eyes flashing, Belle rose. "And by that, I suppose you mean *I* am not good ton?"

"No, no, I don't! Nothing of the kind!" Sir Charles saw his hopes of a romantic interlude slipping away. "Wouldn't even suggest such a thing—you know I wouldn't."

"I don't know anything of the sort," Miss Ryland said grandly. "But I do know I shan't walk with anyone who thinks I'm not good ton. I shall continue on my own.'' Head high, she swept off.

"Belle! Belle, wait!" he called, but she ignored him and he sank back on the log. "Oh, damn it all!" said Sir Charles disgustedly.

Belle's anger carried her forward for some minutes. But there was no one to admire her performance and the path was becoming too overgrown for outraged striding, anyway. She looked expectantly behind her. Really, who would have thought Charles was such a milksop? Well, she certainly wasn't going back to *him*.

The path grew narrower and lost itself in a tangle of undergrowth. The wood was very silent, and Belle thought she had never before noticed how sinister such a place could be. Then there was a rustle by her feet.

Glancing down, Belle thought she saw a thin brown rope wriggling towards her. She shrieked loudly and fled, blundering her way through the bushes.

Ivor had just finished the end of his cigar. It had been a particularly mellow one and had capped a highly satisfactory lunch. He was now making his way back to the elm tree, a rather slow way as he knew ladies of a certain age did not like to be caught napping. And Ivor had his own reasons for keeping on the good side of at least one of these ladies.

There was a crash, then a gasping sob, and Belle hurled herself upon him. In theory, Ivor had no objection to beautiful young women throwing themselves at him, though in practice he preferred that they did not do so with their full weight. He staggered, winded.

"Snake! Snake!" screamed Belle. "Python! Viper! Cobra!"

"Cobra?" Ivor got his breath. "Don't sound right to me—cobra in Dorking Wood."

Belle grasped at his arm and tried to straighten herself, but her foot slipped on some moss and her ankle turned. "Ouch!" She clutched again at Ivor.

He stumbled once more. "Dash it, gel, what is it now? Another cobra?"

"No, no, my ankle."

"Not broken it, have you?"

"I don't think so, but it does hurt."

"Better get you back to the chaise, then. Lean on me."

They could see the others now. Lucinda, Will, Patience and Richard had joined forces and were sitting beneath the spreading elm. Even from halfway across the field, it was possible to see that only Miss Grantham and Mr. Devereux were taking part in any conversation.

Much as Ivor appreciated the role of chivalrous rescuer, he felt Belle's weight even more. "Ho there!" he shouted. "Help ho!"

They came hurrying to meet him and Ivor gladly yielded Belle to her brother's arms. The two duennas were fully awake now and took charge, sending a handkerchief to be soaked in the stream and arranging for Belle to be carefully settled in the chaise.

Dispatched to collect pillows and a rug, Lucinda watched as Patience and Richard fetched a restorative glass of wine for the invalid. They did not, she considered, viciously punching a velvet pillow, they did *not* need to stand quite so close together, or to whisper quite so much.

Sir Charles emerged from the wood and had to have the situation explained to him. His chagrin was complete when his mother, hurrying by with some sal volatile, said accusingly, "Really, Charles, could you not have taken better care of Belle?"

By common consent the excursion was felt to be over. Ivor resigned his seat in the chaise to Belle and joined the two girls in the landau. He paid them a number of bluff, jovial compliments, but when neither responded more than perfunctorily, he soon fell silent.

Dev led the cavalcade and Charles and Will rode beside the landau, but both appeared sunk in gloom. Patience's thoughts also seemed to be less than enlivening. As Lucinda watched the golden afternoon decline, she felt that no one could describe the expedition as a success.

CERTAINLY, if its object had been to cheer Lucinda, it had been a distinct failure. She awoke the next day in the same crotchets. When she and Ethelreda went for a stroll along New Bond Street the next morning, she could scarcely respond patiently to the acquaintances they met, and their endless stream of chit-chat.

"Really, cousin," she complained after the third such encounter. "I had no idea London was so full of tattle-mongers."

"Come, Lucinda! There is no need to react like a Methodist. Naturally people are interested in each other's doings."

"Well, I am not." Lucinda glared ferociously at a befrilled gown in a bow-fronted shop window. "I am not in the least concerned with whom Mr. Richard Devereux may marry."

Mrs. Cleeson stared at her. "Are you quite well, Lucinda? Are you sure you do not have the headache or perhaps a touch of indigestion? I am not convinced those gooseberries last night were entirely ripe."

"My digestion is perfectly sound, cousin."

"You need not hesitate to tell me, child, for I know indigestion does tend to make one crotchety."

Lucinda ground her teeth, but Mrs. Cleeson continued, "For you know, it is quite nonsensical to say people ought not to be interested in Mr. Devereux. His impending marriage is the talk of the town. He is a Devereux, after all. And his uncle—" Mrs. Cleeson flushed "—his uncle has told me that Richard feels it is his duty to his family to marry, which is a very proper sentiment."

Lucinda sniffed disparagingly, but Ethelreda's attention was distracted.

"Oh, dear," cried Mrs. Cleeson, "there is Belle with Miles Stratton. What a tiresome girl she is, to be sure."

A vision in blue and white, with a matching parasol, Belle was coming towards them. The only evidence of her mishap of the previous day was a tiny bandage about her ankle. Miles Stratton was in assiduous attendance and Belle leant heavily upon his arm. Behind them trailed Belle's maid, a doting smile on her broad face.

Ethelreda clucked in annoyance. Realizing that her cousin was seriously annoyed, Lucinda said placatingly, "But Mr. Stratton is not so very bad, is he?"

"He is not at all the sort of person Belle should be encouraging. He is nothing but a rake and everyone knows he is hanging out for a rich wife."

"She does have her maid with her."

"That girl," snapped Mrs. Cleeson with unaccustomed asperity, "that girl couldn't chaperon a mouse."

Ethelreda was indeed put out and their meeting with Belle and Stratton was chilly and stilted. Mrs. Cleeson responded frostily to Miles's flamboyant chatter and kept a disapproving eye on Belle. That young lady was obviously bursting with news that she could not impart under that inescapable regard.

However, as she touched her cheek to Lucinda's in farewell, Belle murmured, "Come this afternoon," and pressed her hand meaningfully.

Lucinda mistrusted that look in Belle's blue eyes. She stared hard at Miss Ryland but met only a bland, guileless smile.

On their return home, Mrs. Cleeson found a letter with the Grantham crest awaiting her. She perused the thick cream sheets with many exclamations and rereadings.

"Here's a coil, Lucinda. Amelia writes that she is called away. Her aunt Dorcas is taken ill. She is as old as the hills, my love, and quite gothic. Amelia hopes to return tomorrow, but in the meantime, she asks me to chaperon Belle and Patience at Almack's tonight."

"I had forgot we are to go there this evening."

"I have told you before, Lucinda, how important is the patronesses' approval. I wish you will not go about saying that you have forgot you received vouchers."

"I shall try to remember," replied Lucinda demurely, not wanting to aggravate her cousin further.

"We must go to the Granthams' immediately after lunch. I wish now we had no afternoon engagements. But I must certainly speak to Sir Charles, and then to Belle and Patience. There are so many..."

Ethelreda fussed throughout the meal and when it was over instantly retired to her room to produce a handful of over-scribbled lists. She shuffled and emended them all the way to Cavendish Square.

On arrival, she asked for Sir Charles, but Lucinda was shown to the drawing room where Will and Patience were sitting together on a confidante. Patience blushed and Will leapt to his feet as Lucinda was announced.

"Goodness," Lucinda said. "Do relax, you two. Who on earth did you think it was?"

"There you are!" Belle hurried in, her ankle apparently completely restored to normal. "Come upstairs right away, Cinda."

But before they could leave, Sir Charles and Mrs. Cleeson entered.

Sir Charles bowed over Lucinda's hand but his eyes were on Belle. "Belle, Mrs. Cleeson wishes to know if you and Patience would prefer to dine with her and Lucinda, before you go to Almack's tonight?"

Belle affected to think. "Why, I believe I would prefer to dine here, you know. It would give us more time to, er, dress. What do you think, Patience?" Lucinda particularly mistrusted Belle's air of innocent deliberation.

"What I should like to know," said Patience, with a teasing look at her brother, "is why Charles says 'when you go Almack's,' as though *he* were not going, too."

Sir Charles glanced uneasily at Will. "It's not that we are not going exactly..." he mumbled.

"We?" Belle cried, "What are you and Will up to?"

"Now, Belle, Grantham and I are just going out of Town for a while."

"A mill! I know you, Will, you're off to some dreadful prize-fight."

"I believe you're right, Belle. Look at their faces!" said Patience, laughing.

"No use trying to hide anything from you ladies," said Charles ruefully. "But we aren't abandoning you and it isn't a 'dreadful' prize-fight. It's a dashed important one.''

"Be back well in time to dance at Almack's," Will promised reassuringly. "Bring our gear with us, you know."

"By Jove, yes. Can't go to Almack's without the proper rig."

"Meet you there, ladies, before you've even had time to miss us."

"Be certain you do." Belle looked sideways at Sir Charles. "If you come too late, our cards will be completely filled and we shan't be able to spare you a dance."

"Miss Ryland," Charles declared dramatically, "if I have to fight a duel to remove one of your partners, a waltz with you will be worth it."

"That's all very well," Mrs. Cleeson interjected, looking up from her lists. "But you do remember, do you not, that the doors will be locked at eleven. Not even the Prince Regent is admitted after that."

"We shan't forget, Mrs. Cleeson. We shall have bags of time."

"Well, we certainly haven't." She rose. "Patience, Belle, we shall call for you this evening. Will, Sir Charles, we shall await you at Almack's. Come, Lucinda, we have calls to make."

"Enjoy yourself at Almack's, Lucinda dear," Belle whispered as they kissed. "I have quite other fish to fry." And Belle smiled seraphically at her.

Lucinda hesitated, staring back at her friend.

"Come, Lucinda," Ethelreda called again in growing impatience.

With a last look at Belle, Lucinda followed her cousin out. They made a number of calls and at last arrived at Lady Borely's. As she munched tiny macaroons and sipped pale, straw-coloured tea, Lucinda's thoughts were still with Belle.

What was that very unreliable girl planning? She placed no faith whatsoever in Belle's discretion and she grew increasingly uneasy as the afternoon wore on.

Lady Borely's teas were select affairs, but their precise observances of propriety and stately manners in no wise impeded the flow of gossip. Lucinda soon found herself joined by Miss Florinda Borely on the yellow sofa.

"And what did you think of the pictures at Somerset House, Miss Neville? Mrs. Cleeson told my mama you had been in attendance."

Lucinda looked down at her tiny cup. She could not really recall what any of the pictures had looked like. "There were a great number of them," she ventured at last.

"Oh, indeed! And such a squeeze! I vow I thought we should never win our way back to the door."

"Many members of the ton were there."

Miss Borely laughed tinklingly. "Quite so. I was much interested to see some of those present." She looked meaningfully at Lucinda.

"Oh?" Miss Neville looked uncomprehendingly back.

Dramatically, Miss Borely lowered her voice. "As we were arriving, Mama met her dear friend Miss Barchester-Trump in the hall outside the Great Room. I was waiting with them when I heard footsteps from one of the side halls, coming from one of the rooms where there are *no exhibitions.*" She emphasized the last words.

Lucinda blinked at her.

"And who do you think it was? All flushed and panting?" She did not wait for an answer. "Lady Chloris dePoer!"

Lucinda's gasp of surprise was all Miss Borely could have wished for.

"You may well stare," she said in satisfaction. "For you know, she gives herself such airs—as though such things as vulgar assignations were far from her thoughts." Florinda laughed mockingly.

"Assignations?" Lucinda's cup rattled on the saucer.

"What else? Of course—" Miss Borely looked virtuous "—I should never have suspected such behaviour if the first person I set eyes upon in the Great Room had not been Richard Devereux! And what else could she have been doing outside the exhibition hall?" She sat back with a triumphant air and gave her attention to a pink marchpane sweetmeat.

"Did I hear you mention Richard Devereux?" Lady Borely leaned towards her daughter. "I believe we are shortly to expect an interesting announcement from that quarter."

Miss Barchester-Trump, a thin, acidulated lady of uncertain years, nodded vigorously. "Yes, yes. I am, you must know, greatly in the confidence of a certain lady," she declared, glancing round to gather everyone's attention. Her listeners all looked knowing, except for Lucinda who was merely baffled. "I have it on the very best of authority—" Miss Barchester-Trump preened herself for a moment, then went on impressively "—that they are merely waiting for Lord dePoer to return from France to make a formal announcement."

A buzz of conversation greeted this intelligence.

"And you, Miss Neville..." Lady Borely looked closely at Lucinda. "I had at one time thought that you...well, you did seem to be on terms of considerable intimacy with Mr. Devereux."

Lucinda put down her cup. "I, Lady Borely? I?"

"Do not be upset, my dear. I realize I was quite mistaken." Her ladyship tapped Lucinda playfully with her fan. "For I see now that you had quite other intentions. We shall soon be hearing another interesting announcement, I don't doubt."

Lucinda flushed scarlet, but fortunately some of the guests were now leaving and Lady Borely and Florinda rose to receive their farewells. Thankfully, Lucinda went to sit beside Mrs. Cleeson for the duration of their visit.

Later, on the way home, Lucinda said, "What was Lady Borely hinting at, cousin Ethelreda?"

Mrs. Cleeson gave her a searching look. "Well, it has been rather remarked, Lucinda dearest."

"What has, cousin?"

"That you are much in Will's company."

"Oh!" To her chagrin Lucinda found herself flushing again.

"You do not need to be upset, dearest. After all, it is not unknown for childhood friends to discover they are becoming something closer." Mrs. Cleeson patted her charge's hand.

In confusion, Lucinda gazed out at the London streets. She had not told Mrs. Cleeson of her secret engagement and was curiously taken aback to find that her cousin and at least Lady Borely suspected an understanding. She was glad when the carriage drew up at Agincourt Circle and Mrs. Cleeson hurried her upstairs to rest.

"You must be in your best looks tonight, you know, for it will be your first appearance at Almack's," her cousin reminded her before retiring for her own nap.

Lucinda thought about crying off that evening. After all she had no use for the Marriage Mart. She knew a rebellious urge to fly in the face of convention, which only turned her thoughts to Belle and all her worries about her friend returned. She kicked off her shoes and lay down on the bed.

Disturbing recollections of Belle's past escapades flashed through her mind. In Nether Wilden these had been indulgently regarded as a mere excess of high spirits. But Lucinda knew the reaction would not be so tolerant in Town, and she was dreadfully afraid that Belle was plotting something.

She glanced up and saw that Emmie had propped a letter up on her dressing-table. It must have been delivered when she was out. She reached over and snatched it up. But her face fell as she read it.

She had written earlier to Mr. Bunthorpe, enquiring as to the progress of Freddie Simms, the boy she and Mr. Devereux had taken to the hospice. Now Mr. Bunthorpe had responded, presenting his compliments and begging leave to inform Miss Neville that Mr. Devereux had taken care of the matter.

"Whatever that means," Lucinda muttered, dropping the single sheet, and immediately fell back to fretting over Belle.

She lay down again, but she could not rest. She picked up a book but was unable to concentrate. Finally, she sat up and rang the bell. When Emmie appeared, Lucinda sent her to order the coach.

CHAPTER TEN

THE NIGHT OF the Vernissage, Richard Devereux sat in his library. There was a glass of sherry in his hand and a tray of plain biscuits and walnuts beside him. His gleaming Hessians were planted firmly on the fender of the Italian marble fireplace and his gaze was fixed above on the painting by Stubbs.

It showed two horses being led out of the stable. Mr. Devereux had owned the picture for some ten years now and he had been staring steadily at it for the past half hour. It would have been a safe wager, however, that once interrupted, he could not have said what he was so intently regarding.

"Hope I don't disturb you, neffy."

Devereux brought his feet down with a thump. "Ivor!"

"Told Larrigan I'd announce myself. In a brown study, eh?"

"I was thinking," Richard said with dignity, sitting straighter in his chair.

"Oh, aye, aye. I don't doubt it. Marriage takes a bit of thought, after all."

"Much you know about it," his nephew responded tartly. He turned to pour a drink for Ivor and so did not see that his uncle's colour had darkened.

"Ah, well, Ricky," he said with excessive heartiness, "live and learn, you know, live and learn."

Dev handed him the glass and came back to his seat. "Haven't seen much of you recently, Ivor." He recalled Charles's remark. "Been spending a lot of time at Agincourt Circle, have you?"

"Harrumph!" Ivor drank deeply. "Now, now, my boy. No harm in visiting a lady—old friend, you know, lots to catch up on."

"I didn't know you had any lady friends, old or otherwise. Not much in the petticoat line, didn't you say?"

"Dash it all, Ricky! Don't take a fellow up so sharp." He took another gulp. "Damme if I don't think you're getting more like your father every day. And a dashed nasty tongue he had, too."

Dev laughed. "What a crushing thing to say, Ivor—to compare me to my late and quite unlamented sire."

"Well, I don't say you're entirely like him, but you want to take care, my boy."

"I shall watch myself for any such signs."

"You do that. But tell me, Ricky, how are matters progressing with the fair Chloris?"

"Have you a wager on it, dear uncle?"

"Bet you wouldn't go through with it." Ivor answered so promptly and shamelessly that Dev was forced to laugh again. "But I don't mind dropping a few guineas, provided you're satisfied."

"Ivor," said Dev, moved, "that is uncommonly handsome of you and in return I shall tell you that I have not made any offer to anyone as yet."

"Can't screw your courage to the sticking-point?" Ivor grinned and poured himself another drink. "Ought to ask Charles for advice. He's made no secret of his affection for the Ryland chit." He wriggled his back reminiscently. "Dashed fine-looking girl but a bit on the hefty side."

Dev smiled. "I saw him at Somerset House this afternoon. I'm surprised they didn't snatch him up to model for the life classes—some of his poses deserve to be immortalized."

"You, at the Vernissage? Ethelreda didn't mention seeing you."

"I didn't know Mrs. Cleeson, and I suppose Miss Neville, were there."

"In the thick of it, from what I hear."

Dev's attention had apparently returned to his Stubbs and the even tenor of his voice did not vary as he remarked, "From what I hear, there will be another marriage in the Ryland family."

"Lucinda and the young fellow, you mean?"

"So I've heard."

"They've known each other forever, so I collect," Ivor said, frowning. "Ethelreda says it's common for such close acquaintances to change their feelings. But I don't know, they don't strike me as nutty on each other."

"No?" Dev had risen and now stood with his back to Ivor as though to get a closer view of the painted horses. "They seem much in each other's company."

"Whole crew of 'em go about together—Ryland and his sister, Charles and his sister and Lucinda."

"Well then, Ivor, are we to expect an announcement soon?"

Ivor jerked his hand back from the biscuit tray and sent his glass tottering. He caught it just in time. "Here, steady on, Ricky. What do you mean by springing a question like that on a fellow?"

Dev turned and raised his eyebrow. "But, Ivor, I merely enquired if we are to expect an announcement of an engagement between young Ryland and Miss Neville. That is what we are discussing, is it not?"

"Oh, *that.* None planned that I know of. Ethelreda has some doubts that the gel's fixed her interest in that way. The coming-out ball's to take place shortly and Jasper Neville's due in Town for that. Ryland will have to speak to him, and from what Ethelreda says, he's dashed protective of his only chick."

Mr. Devereux resumed his seat and sprawled at his ease. "Have you dined yet, Ivor?"

"No, but I just dropped in—"

"Then you must dine with me." He touched the bell pull. "And I shall tell Larrigan to bring up several bottles of the burgundy you are so fond of."

"Thankee, neffy, thankee. But what's the occasion?"

Dev smiled seraphically. "Let's just say, my dear uncle, that it is because I am so very glad to see you."

MR. DEVEREUX rose earlier than was his wont the next morning. However, Dowsett remained unperturbed even when his master requested him to send a footman for a hackney.

After a quick breakfast then, Devereux leapt into the coach and ordered the driver to make for the Isle of Dogs. As he went through the gates of the hospice, he could hear the happy shouts of children sporting on the grass. He paid the hackney driver, then stood for a moment to watch them.

Their faces were bright, but he noted their thin bodies and pale cheeks. He was frowning when he finally went inside to meet Mr. Bunthorpe.

"How many children do you have here now?" he asked after the formalities had been exchanged.

"Counting your young Master Simms, there are five at present."

"And their ailments?"

"Two are accident victims and the others..." Mr Bunthorpe continued with a sigh, "their parents call it the 'wasting fever.' I should say it is a combination of insufficient food, unsanitary conditions and too much responsibility too soon."

"It is damnable!" Devereux burst out. "More must be done!"

"I cannot argue with you there. But we are making progress. This hospice is one sign. Your interest and the interest of other persons of station and property is another."

"It seems so little."

"Perhaps. But I must mention that we hope also to persuade the government to act. There is some talk of an enquiry into the workings of the Poor Laws. Reform in that line would be of inestimable value in work such as ours."

"There I can be of some assistance, for in that area I have some influence."

"Any increase in awareness would be a blessing."

"We shall speak more of this, Mr. Bunthorpe. But now, tell me how my young friend does."

"He is in better pin, but again, rest, good food, clean air help him now. But to what shall we send him back?"

"There, too," Devereux said with decision, "I may be of use. May I see him?"

"Certainly." Mr. Bunthorpe consulted his watch. "He should just be finishing some milk and bread now. Let me take you to him."

They went along a stone path bordered by red geraniums to where a spreading elm shaded the river bank. Seated on a blanket, the children were holding tin mugs and plates. A blue-coated attendant was handing out thick slabs of buttered bread.

Mr. Bunthorpe greeted him politely and asked if Master Simms could be excused. The attendant smiled and gestured to a freckle-faced, round-eyed boy.

"This is Mr. Devereux, Freddie," the warden said. "He would like to speak to you. Perhaps you might sit on the bench." He gestured to an old wooden seat a little farther off.

Freddie cast a wary look at his visitor and rather reluctantly rose. He did, however, manage to snaffle a thick slice before trailing after Devereux. Chewing steadily, he sat rather suspiciously at the far end of the seat.

"It weren't my fault," he said automatically.

"No," agreed Dev calmly.

Freddie's eyes grew rounder and he masticated more slowly. "I couldn't help it."

"I was entirely at fault. I must beg you to forgive me."

Freddie was so surprised he forgot to chew. He stared unwinkingly at Mr. Devereux, swallowed convulsively and said, "That's all right, then."

"You are not a London man?" Devereux asked conversationally.

"How'd you know?"

"You sound more like someone from my part of the country."

"Are you from Dorset then, sir?"

"Devon, actually."

"Ah." Freddie nodded knowledgeably. "My pa were in Devon once."

"That was before you came to London?"

"Us only came to Lunnon three months ago."

"And do you like it?" Devereux asked carefully, keeping all emotion from his voice.

Freddie's face clouded. "It's fine," he mumbled, "us be doing fine."

Mr. Devereux took a deep interest in a scull on the river. "Oh?" he said. "I asked, you know, because I had a suggestion to make."

Freddie studied the boat also. He finished the last of his milk and, eyes still on the river, said with elaborate disinterest, "What be that, sir?"

"I have a house in Devon and I am in need of some help."

"Truly?" Freddie's pose of indifference vanished. "You're not just bamming me?"

"No, Freddie," he replied gently. "I am quite serious. Tell me, what is your father's work?"

"He's a farm hand, sir—a prime shepherd. He knows everything about sheep. But his old master, he decided to rent out his land and there weren't work for Pa anymore."

"So you came to London?"

"Us heard there's work for everyone in Lunnon."

"And has your pa found work?" Dev's voice was even more gentle.

"He has that, in one of them man-u-factories. But—" Freddie blinked rapidly "—it's too hard, sir. My mam says so and he coughs now, all the time. My mam says he's got to get some good Dorchester air."

Devereux rested his hand briefly on the boy's thin shoulder and tactfully ignored the stifled sob. "I expect your mam is perfectly right and I promise that when Mr. Bunthorpe says you are well, you shall all travel to Devon together."

"And live in the country again?" At Dev's answering nod, a wide grin spread across Freddie's freckled face. "Why, sir, that's ... that's *prime!*"

Mr. Devereux was smiling when he left the hospice and summoned a hackney. But his smile dimmed as he came nearer to his destination. The driver looked dubious as he paid him off and strode down the filthy, narrow street.

It was not the first time Devereux had visited such areas and, as always, a cold anger seized him as he hastened on. The air was foetid here, but he did not reach for a handkerchief and he allowed no hint of his feelings to show upon his face.

Freddie had given him careful directions, so there must be an alley here. Yes, though "alley" was perhaps too grand a word for such a wretched opening. But here was the door Freddie had described. It was distinguished from its neighbours only by a lack of debris in front. He knocked and the door was opened by a thin, grey-haired woman in a neat apron.

"Mrs. Simms?" he asked. "I am Richard Devereux. I've just come from visiting Freddie."

A look of near panic crossed her weary face. "Oh, sir, Freddie's a good boy. I'm sure he never meant no harm."

"I know that, Mrs. Simms. I have not come to complain. May I come in?"

Mutely, Mrs. Simms gestured him into the one room. It obviously functioned as kitchen, dining room and bedroom. It was plainly, indeed sparsely, furnished. But it was clean and extremely neat. Mrs.

Simms took one straight wooden chair and Devereux the only other.

"You don't blame Freddie, then?" she asked, as though hesitant to believe him.

"It was altogether my fault," he repeated firmly. "So I have come to offer you what recompense I may."

"I'm sure Simms and I don't want any such thing, sir."

"But it would be a great help to me if you accepted and I'm persuaded it would be good for Freddie."

"Freddie?" Mrs. Simms's drawn face lightened.

"And for your husband, who I believe," he added gently, "is not well."

Her shoulders sagged. "No," she said dully, "he's not."

"Then," Devereux went on in the same tone, "I wonder if you and your family would consider working for me. I have estates in Devon and we are always looking for reliable workers."

"Oh, sir!" Mrs. Simms's face was transformed. "Do you mean, go back to the country?" Her words echoed her son's.

"If you would, Mrs. Simms."

"Oh, sir!" Overcome, she reached out and grasped his hand. "That I would!"

Dev disentangled his hand. He reached into his pocket and placed a fat purse on the scrubbed wooden table. "You will have expenses to cover when you remove to Devon, so pray accept this—"

he looked at Mrs. Simms "—shall we say as an advance, to ease your way."

Mrs. Simms blinked rapidly, then mastered herself. "I—I can't say what this means to us, sir. And Simms!" She smiled, suddenly looking years younger. "Ah, sir, what'll Simms say when he hears! Now," she said, bustling over to some uneven shelves. "You'll take some refreshment, I hope?"

He would not hurt her feelings by refusing as he pulled the chair to the table. Carefully, Mrs. Simms poured from a bottle into a cup.

"That's good Dorset cider, sir. Us brought it with us, us did." She took half a loaf from the shelf and cut it into thin slices. These she arranged on a blue-and-white plate and placed beside him.

He ate two pieces of the coarse bread, reflecting bitterly that it was probably the only food in the house. However, at least he'd made sure she had money to buy more.

He discussed the moving with Mrs. Simms as he ate. It was arranged that he would send a carriage to take her to the hospice tomorrow. There she and Mr. Bunthorpe would discuss when it would be permissible for Freddie to make the long journey south.

"But you need not wonder about that," he said as he rose, "for whenever the warden says he may travel, I shall send a travelling coach for you and you yourselves shall set the pace of your journey."

With Mrs. Simms's thanks ringing in his ears, Devereux stepped out again into the stifling air. His face settled into a grim expression as he strode unseeing through the crowded, filthy streets.

That's three saved, he thought to himself as he marched. But it was too few, always too few. And he could not take everyone to work for him in Devon. He recalled Mr. Bunthorpe's words. Yes, he must speak to those parliamentarians he knew. He could even manage a chat with the Prime Minister. And a word in Prinny's ear wouldn't go amiss, either.

Then there was Jasper Neville's idea: to get more of the ton involved. He could approach some of his friends; even Charles might be interested. He'd have to pick the right moment there, though. Preferably one when Miss Belle Ryland was far, far away.

He remembered Ivor's comment about a wife not countenancing such an interest. But surely that need not be true? There must be some females who would care for more than clothes and dances. For instance, someone like, well, Lucinda Neville. Now, with a woman like that, one who shared truly in his interests, marriage could be a real partnership.

Absorbed in his own thoughts, Mr. Devereux found himself already in the Strand; a hackney driver's shouted curse brought him to himself in the middle of the thoroughfare. Making placating gestures, he hurried to the other side.

What on earth had he been thinking? Daydreaming, in truth! At his age! Rather guiltily Dev adjusted his hat and hailed another coach. He settled himself inside and this time he kept his mind firmly on the task of marshalling his influence—and no nonsense about females was allowed to intrude.

CHAPTER ELEVEN

WHEN SHE REACHED the Grantham house, Lucinda was informed that Miss Ryland had already left. The butler made his regrets, but he could not say where Miss Ryland had gone. He looked mournfully at Lucinda as he spoke.

"Very well, then." Lucinda was shaken, but she spoke calmly. "Send her maid to me, please."

The butler nodded and withdrew. He must know something was amiss, Lucinda realized, otherwise he would not have acceded so readily to such an irregular request.

Mabel came slowly into the room. She was uneasy, and Lucinda could see that she was also worried.

"Now, Mabel," Lucinda said firmly. "You know this is a serious matter. Where is your mistress?"

"Oh, miss, I promised I wouldn't tell . . ."

"You know it is your duty to protect Miss Ryland. She has not considered the consequences of her actions. But we must. Where is she?"

"Oh, miss! She's gone to dinner with Mr. Stratton and afterwards he's taking her to one of them gambling places—hells, they call them."

"A *hell?*" Lucinda gripped the back of a chair. "Belle has gone to a gambling den?"

"I did tell her that she oughtn't . . ."

"I should certainly think you might!" Lucinda took a few agitated steps. "What can Belle be thinking of? Suppose she were to be seen? And tonight, when she is supposed to be at Almack's. Oh, she puts me quite out of curl!"

Mabel broke into noisy sobs. "She'll be ruined, miss. Whatever can we do?" she wailed.

Lucinda stopped pacing. "Where is Sir Charles?"

"He's at St. Albans, miss. He and Mr. Ryland left after luncheon."

"That wretched mill! And Will with him!" Lucinda pressed her hands to her forehead. "I must think."

Someone must get Belle back before she sank herself utterly beyond recall. But that someone could not be Lucinda, even if she had any idea where such an establishment could be found. If only Papa were here!

But he wasn't. She would have to cope on her own. Unless . . . Suddenly Lucinda felt quite giddy with relief. Of course, the very person!

"Pray stop that noise, Mabel," she said as she began to pull on her gloves. "I want you to listen to me. Go upstairs and lay out the clothes your mistress is to wear at Almack's tonight. She will have to dress very quickly when she returns. And make sure that no one else hears of this adventure."

She went swiftly back to her own carriage. "Twenty-five Agincourt Crescent," she told the coachman.

With a sigh she settled against the squabs. Mr. Devereux would help; he would undoubtedly know the hell and what to do. Lucinda did not question her confidence in his ability. Her thoughts were entirely concerned with calculations of time. Would there enough of it? Could Belle be saved in spite of herself?

However, when at last Larrigan opened the door to her, she realized how odd her actions must appear. It was highly unusual for an unaccompanied young lady to visit a gentleman at such an hour.

"I should like to speak with Mr. Devereux, please," Lucinda said with as much authority as she could muster. She remembered Mr. Bunthorpe's letter and lifted her chin. "I wish to consult him on...on the boy who was injured," she finished in a rush. She knew she did not need to offer an explanation to the butler, but nervousness prompted her to justify her actions.

Larrigan was an excellent butler, and if he considered this visit highly unconventional, he did not permit this to show in his manner. "This way, miss," he said expressionlessly.

Her face flaming, Lucinda followed him to the library.

"I shall inform Mr. Devereux that you are here," he said, then bowed and left her there, perched on the edge of an enormous wing-chair and prey to the most lowering fears and misgivings.

Upstairs, Mr. Devereux was preparing for Almack's. For many years he had not frequented that establishment, but tonight he had promised to see Lady dePoer and Chloris there. Charles had told him that the Grantham party would also be in attendance, so he supposed that perhaps Miss Neville would be with them. He wondered if she had had that gold lace made up yet. With that hair and those eyes the effect should be...

He wrenched his thoughts back to a proper direction. He had paid constant attentions to Chloris and neither she nor her mother could be ignorant of the rumours circulating among the ton. Lord dePoer was away on a diplomatic mission, but his wife must be in daily expectation of a declaration from Mr. Devereux.

It was this declaration which he was discussing with Dowsett. "After all, as my Aunt Melpond has pointed out, a man in my station cannot be so foolish as to hold out for a love-match."

The valet occupied himself with the sleeves of his master's shirt. When these were to his satisfaction, he picked up the white satin waistcoat.

Richard held out his arms. "The whole idea of falling in love must, of course, be dismissed as a piece of romantical nonsense and I am long past the age for such folly. Do you not agree, Dowsett?"

Directly appealed to, Dowsett produced a sound halfway between a snort and a grunt. Whether it signified agreement or otherwise, it satisfied Mr. Devereux.

"Exactly so. Such notions belong to the melodramas so favoured by Sir Charles. And I cannot envy the Cheltenham tragedies he and Miss Ryland have been enacting. No, the matter must be regarded in a sensible and down-to-earth way." He sat down to put on the buckle shoes to go with the knee breeches demanded by Almack's. "After all, Dowsett, you must recall my parents' marriage. That was supposed to be the love-match of their generation and you do not need me to remind you to what bitterness and recrimination that very soon sank."

"Your pardon, sir." Larrigan stood at the door. "But Miss Neville had called."

"Miss Neville?" Devereux held still and stared at him.

"Yes, sir. I understand her to be desirous of discussing the young person who was injured."

"Freddie Simms?" Dev repeated blankly. "But that matter is all settled." He reached for his paisley silk dressing-gown. "I shall be down directly, Larrigan."

Lucinda jumped up as soon as he entered the library. "Mr. Devereux! Thank heavens! I have been so worried."

He took her hands and said, scanning her face, "Miss Neville, I cannot think you should be here. You need not agitate yourself over young Freddie. He and his family are to go to Beacon End, my house in Devon. I intended to discuss this all with you as soon as I next saw you."

He was still holding her hands and she knew she should withdraw them, but it was so very comforting to feel his touch. "It's Belle—Miss Ryland. I do not know what it is best to do."

He drew her down to the sofa and took both her hands in one of his own, as he pulled the bell. "I know that you must have some refreshment before you go any further. You look wretchedly shocked."

"No, please, I don't—"

"But I think you do. Come now, Miss Neville." He smiled hearteningly at her. "Nothing will be gained if you faint on me again."

Lucinda laughed shakily, but the brandy, when it came, did calm her nerves, and as clearly as she could, she told her story.

Mr. Devereux drew his straight brows together. "Miles Stratton? I have seen her flirt with him, of course, but I had not thought . . ."

"I am sure she cares nothing for him. It is just that she does not consider. And she and Charles had that quarrel in the wood. Do you know where he may have taken her, sir?"

"I can make a good guess. Stratton is a here-and-therian, but he's no stretchhalter. The only possible hell for such an escapade is Lucy Caldeane's. It is much frequented by the ton."

"But surely no lady goes there!"

"No lady," he said and his emphasis made Lucinda flush. "What can be done?" she cried. "I

cannot stand idly by and let Belle ruin herself forever.''

Richard rose. ''I think perhaps that matters may
not be as serious as you imagine. It is quite common
for guests at Lucy's to be masked. It is, you might
say, one of the trademarks of her house. I don't
doubt Stratton has insisted Miss Ryland follow the
custom.''

''But anyone could recognize that hair.''

''Possibly,'' said Mr. Devereux coolly. ''But it is
still very early in the evening. The company will be
very thin and I doubt many members of the ton will
arrive till very much later.''

''Pray God there is no one else there.''

''That, I'm afraid, is rather too unlikely, but those
there at such an hour may not recognize your
friend.'' He came to stand before her. He held out his
hand and shyly Lucinda put hers into it. ''Miss Neville, you must return home now. Are you engaged for
this evening?''

''Yes, at Almack's, and Belle should be there,
too.''

''Gently now. I shall come to you there, as soon as
I may. Go now. Get dressed. Stand buff. I promise
you we shall come round.'' He raised her hands to his
lips and kissed them.

WHEN SHE HAD made her way home, Lucinda was
surprised to find that her cousin was just waking and
unaware that her charge had been out. It seemed an
age to her since she had been in her own room and

she was almost surprised to find everything unchanged.

But Emmie had been increasingly anxious and immediately rushed Lucinda into a bath and then into a wrapper for the coiffeur. As she was to wear the new gold lace dress, Emmie spread the gold star pins on the dressing table for Monsieur Arnaud.

They seemed to inspire him, for he drew her hair into two cascading bunches over each ear, with only the wispiest tendrils resting on her white forehead. Artfully, he hid the stars in the long ringlets, so they were only half-visible and sparkled intriguingly when she turned her head.

When the highly satisfied Monsieur Arnaud had left, Emmie began the final preparations. Lucinda slipped into the pale gold satin underdress. Then at last Emmie eased the gold lace gown over her head.

It had tiny puff sleeves, a square-necked bodice that clung tight to the bosom and then it fell gracefully to the ground. Her gloves and slippers were of matching gold satin. Around her neck and on one wrist she wore fine gold chains, interspersed with tiny amber beads.

"Most elegant, dearest," approved cousin Ethelreda, who was looking particularly handsome in burgundy lutestring. "Célie was quite right to keep everything simple, so nothing distracts from the colour."

Staring at herself in the looking-glass, Lucinda turned slowly about. It was hard to believe that sophisticated young woman was really she. She looked

so much older and somehow more...more knowing. And could that be a touch of sadness in the huge
brown eyes?

I wonder what Will will think of this dress, she
thought idly. Then, with much more intensity, *I do
hope it pleases Mr. Devereux.*

Patience was waiting for them at Cavendish
Square. She looked delightfully fresh in rose pink,
with the Grantham pearls at her throat.

"And where is Belle?" demanded Mrs. Cleeson.

"She...she is not well," Patience said haltingly.
She glanced quickly at Lucinda and then away.

"Not well?" repeated Ethelreda ominously.
"Have you sent for the doctor?"

"Please, Mrs. Cleeson, do not ask me any more
questions. Belle will join as at Almack's in just a little while, I'm sure."

Mrs. Cleeson studied her for a moment. "Belle is
not here? I see." There was a pause. "Well, Patience, I must bring you and Lucinda to Almack's
and I have no intention of being late. I collect Belle
is in some scrape, but if she does not soon appear, I
shall have to know far more about it. And I cannot
reconcile it with my conscience to keep any of this
from your mama."

In silence the party continued on its way to the
Assembly Rooms. Lucinda had been warned to
expect genteel shabbiness, but tonight she took little
notice of her surroundings. She tried to keep within
sight of the entry, but the number of people in-

creased and Mrs. Cleeson propelled her relentlessly forward.

The night should have been a triumph for Lucinda. She attracted many admiring looks and she had no lack of partners. Even when she was introduced to Mrs. Drummond-Burrell, that most top-lofty of the patronesses remarked in supercilious tones that the gown was quite "becoming." She added that if Miss Neville wished, she might join in the waltz.

"Thank goodness for that," declared Ethelreda with a sigh, when Patience had received the same permission. "For you know Mrs. Drummond-Burrell is so extremely nice in her notions that there is no knowing to what she may take exception."

Lucinda noticed that Patience also stared anxiously towards the door. So she, too, had talked to Mabel. To Lucinda, time seemed to speed past. Now there was less than an hour and a half left. What was happening at that hell?

Beside her, Patience gave a gasp. "Here they are!"

Lucinda's pulse raced and she looked up, but it was only Will and Sir Charles. Will saw them instantly and began to make his way towards them. Lucinda's partner claimed her and Will swept Patience onto the dance floor.

Sir Charles had been detained by the Countess Lieven. His eyes scanned the crowd, but his scowl grew fiercer as he failed to see Belle. He escaped the countess and was waiting for Lucinda as the dance ended.

"Where is Belle?" he demanded unceremoniously.

"Miss Ryland," said Lucinda with a calmness she did not feel, "has been delayed and will arrive shortly."

"It's another one of her starts, isn't it? I demand that you tell me where she is."

"Please moderate your voice, Sir Charles. People are beginning to stare."

Charles reddened. "I am sorry, Miss Neville. Pray forgive me. But I knew Belle was up to something from the way she was behaving this afternoon. She cannot deceive me. I should never have gone to that mill."

Truth to tell, Lucinda rather wished he hadn't also, but there was little point in bemoaning the past. "Never mind, Sir Charles, I'm sure Belle will be here in no time." *If only Mr. Devereux is able to find her,* she added silently to herself.

Charles accepted her assurances with a good grace and asked her to dance. As they struggled across the floor in Charles's usual style, Lucinda felt again some stirrings of sympathy for Belle's interest in Miles Stratton.

Sir Charles was an abominable dancer; he plunged and swooped, accelerated rapidly, just as unaccountably slowed down and swung his hapless partner in unexpected turns. Lucinda hung on and hoped they would not career into any of the more sedate couples.

Suddenly, Charles drew in his breath and intoned, "Aah!" It was a sound Lucinda felt would
have done justice to Mr. Keane himself in Drury
Lane. But she followed his gaze. To her amazement
and relief, she beheld Lady Grantham and there, behind her, demurely clad in peach sarsenet and smiling sweetly, was Belle.

The music ceased and Sir Charles, muttering ex-
cuses, left her and began shouldering his way towards his mother and her charge.

"The prodigal returns," drawled a voice behind
her and Mr. Devereux was beside her at last.

"Mr. Devereux! How glad I am to see you!" Lucinda's velvet eyes glowed in the candlelight. "Thank
you, thank you, thank you!"

"Hush, Miss Neville." His own glance was just as
warm. "Have you permission to waltz?" At her nod,
he whirled her into his arms. For the first time that
evening, Lucinda was conscious of a man's arm
about her waist and of her body responding to the
music—and to him. For the first time, too, she began to understand why some people still considered
the waltz a scandalous dance.

"And Lady Grantham is here, too," she said.
"However did you manage that?"

"It was none of my doing, but I collect her relative has recovered more quickly than was expected."

"But what has happened? I have been so worried."

His grip tightened and he looked down into her
upturned face for a long moment. "I was right about

the gold lace," he said softly. "You are very beautiful, Lucinda. Did you know that there are gold flecks in your eyes?"

Lucinda's breathing quickened. He had used her name! "But, but, about Belle..." Her throat was dry and she had trouble keeping her voice steady.

"You are right, as usual. This is not the time. Miss Ryland? I found her in Lucy's, all right."

Hideous memories of past scenes when Belle had been thwarted rose before her. "Was she very difficult?" she asked apprehensively.

"Not at all," said the Beau coolly. "In fact, I flatter myself that she may even have been rather glad to see me."

"Was it so very dreadful a place?"

"It wasn't the place."

Lucinda clutched at his coat. "Good heavens! Was it Mr. Stratton? Did he...?"

Gently, he removed her grip. "Miss Neville, I will do anything for you, except permit you to spoil my coat." Lucinda chuckled as he regained her hand. "No, no, in his own way, Stratton is a gentleman. More important for us, however, he is a gambler. A crony of his challenged him to a most elaborate card game. I confess the rules of it baffled me, but it was of consuming interest to Stratton."

Lucinda glanced up through her long lashes. "Can you mean," she asked, a laugh trembling in her voice, "that Stratton was *ignoring* Belle?"

"Ignoring her?" Dev repeated reflectively. "No, I couldn't say he was able to ignore her exactly. Miss

Ryland had embarked upon a comprehensive denunciation of his actions, his character, his probable antecedents and his undoubted end. I will say this for Stratton, though—he didn't let it interfere with his game.''

This time Lucinda did laugh. ''Poor Belle!''

''So, as you may imagine, Miss Ryland was grateful to be rescued from her neglectful escort. Stratton did look up from his hand to bid her goodbye, but she did not appear to appreciate this concession. Fortunately, Lady Grantham arrived just as I delivered Miss Ryland home. She seemed perfectly to grasp the situation, so I left your friend in her capable hands.''

The music ended, but Mr. Devereux did not let go her hand. He drew her aside into one of the alcoves. He himself stood with his back to the dancing guests, but, as she stood a little to one side, Lucinda could see straight into the room. She saw Lady Chloris joining the waltz, in the arms of a clearly overawed young man. She flinched and edged away from Mr. Devereux.

''What is it, Lucinda?'' Richard's voice was caressing. ''You came to me, my dear. I was touched, deeply honoured by your trust, for you must know—''

''No! No!'' Lucinda shrank farther away, staring at him out of huge, tear-dimmed eyes.

''What is it? What has happened?''

She groped blindly in her reticule. ''You cannot. You mustn't.'' Her fingers closed on what she was searching for. She forced herself to say the words she must. "I am promised to another." She choked as she pushed the brooch into his hands. "As are you." And Lucinda turned her back and fled from him.

CHAPTER TWELVE

BLINKING BACK HOT TEARS, Lucinda sought sanctuary in the chaperons' corner. There Mrs. Cleeson was enjoying another comfortable cose with Ivor Devereux. Their tiny gilt chairs were pulled close together and their voices low. However, when Lucinda appeared, Ethelreda looked up with a start.

"Ah, Lucinda," she said, hastily stowing away a pencil and yet another list. "Did you see that Belle has finally arrived? And Amelia? What a mercy that is. I have just been telling Ivor that Belle needs at least three chaperons to keep rein on her."

Ivor laughed. "All pretty gels keep their duennas hopping, eh, Miss Neville?"

Lucinda laughed dutifully. She had hoped to persuade her cousin to leave right away, but it was clear Mrs. Cleeson was going to be fully occupied for some time to come. Nervously she looked about. But surely Mr. Devereux would not come after her? She jumped when she felt a touch on her arm.

"Here you are at last," said Belle. "I've been looking for you. I've so much to tell you." If Belle was the prodigal daughter, she didn't look in the least repentant. Her eyes sparkled and she seemed to be thoroughly enjoying herself. "What a perfectly gorgeous gown that is, Lucinda. Gold lace! And your hair! I must get Monsieur Arnaud to try that style for me. You take the shine out of us all tonight."

"Don't be absurd, Belle," Lucinda responded brusquely and Belle blinked at her. "I'm sorry," she said, passing a hand over her forehead. "It's just that I was so worried and it is so hot in here. I must be getting the headache."

"It is terribly hot," Belle agreed. "And I want to talk to you in quiet, anyway." She leaned over to speak to Ethelreda. "Mrs. Cleeson, Lucinda and I are going to one of the withdrawing rooms. We are rather overheated."

"Yes, my dears, do." Mrs. Cleeson was engrossed in Ivor's story. "Almack's can be very stuffy."

The girls skirted the ballroom and, passing the refreshment room, came out into a narrow corridor.

"It's much cooler here already," said Belle. "I believe there is a ladies' room just down here." She wrinkled her nose as she looked about. "I cannot think why Almack's must be so shoddy. Look, the paint is positively peeling. One must hope there will be chairs in the withdrawing room."

Lucinda fanned her flaming cheeks. "All I hope is that it may have a window we can open."

"Oh, no!" Belle had stopped and was examining the bottom of her gown.

"What is it?"

"It's my hem. It's come down." Belle giggled. "I'm not surprised, really. I was dancing with Charles and he trod on it twice. He is a wretched dancer." She giggled again.

"I haven't any pins with me, do you?"

"No, but Lady Grantham or Mrs. Cleeson will. I shall just run back and ask them. Do you go and sit down, Lucinda, for I vow you look quite flushed."

Lucinda watched as Belle hitched her skirts up in a manner that Lady Grantham would surely deplore and ran off. Feeling that she herself would be glad to sit down and gather her thoughts, she opened the nearest door.

It was not a ladies' room. In fact, it looked as though it had been set aside for the use of the musicians. There were instrument cases strewn about, and trays of half-eaten food and wine.

But Lucinda saw none of these. In the middle of the room, with his back to her, stood a tall man with bright red hair. She had never seen him before. But he clasped in his arms and ardently kissed a lady whom Lucinda did recognize. There could be no mistaking that spun-gold hair or those diamonds. She would have known Chloris dePoer anywhere.

Transfixed, she stared at them. The lovers paid no attention to her. She doubted they had heard the door open. Lucinda swayed dizzily and the blood roared in her ears.

She pulled the door closed and stumbled along the hall. She almost fell through the first open door and sank into the nearest chair. "C and R" the brooch had said, but that man was not Richard Devereux. The Ice Queen, they called Chloris, but there had been nothing icy in the way she was responding to those caresses.

And Richard...Lucinda's heart ached for him. He had taken such care over that love-token. How he must have anticipated Chloris's delight. And she— she had cared so little for it and for him that she had dropped it carelessly to the ground—and now she had slipped away from the dancing to meet the red-haired stranger in the other room.

Of course Lucinda knew what went on in Society. She had heard, even if she had not quite believed, all the scandals. But somehow it was different when one knew the people involved and could see who was going to be hurt.

What would I think, Lucinda asked herself, *if I found Will kissing someone else?* She tried to summon up the requisite sense of outrage and betrayal, but she was unmoved by the picture she conjured up. It was really Richard her sympathy went out to. It was his feelings she could most vividly feel, his hurt she most desperately wanted to assuage. She sat staring ahead, her hands working feverishly in her lap.

"Lucinda, whatever is the matter? You look as though you've seen a ghost." It was Belle, back with a small étui in her hand.

Lucinda pulled herself together. "Shall I pin the hem for you? You may stand on this footstool."

Belle looked closely at her friend as she handed over the needle-case. But Lucinda kept her head bent as she worked. She made herself concentrate on the simple manual task and gradually her breathing slowed and her colour grew more normal. By the time the hem was finished, she had achieved tolerable control over her face and feelings.

"Thank you," Belle said as she jumped down and slid her feet back into her Denmark satin slippers. "Though, if I dance with Charles again I daresay it will all be for naught."

"Really, Belle, you are lucky that anyone at all will dance with you. Consider what would have happened if anyone had seen you at that dreadful place."

"Pooh! No one even looked at me—except, of course, Mr. Devereux and he won't tell."

"And what do you think Sir Charles would say if he knew?"

"Charles? I can manage Charles. Naturally he would fly into the most terrible rage and make the most monstrous scene, too, I shouldn't wonder. He does look so handsome when he's angry, don't you think? But he'd forgive me. He always will."

"What odious self-satisfaction, Belle. It gives me quite a disgust of you, to hear you say such things. You are very lucky you came out of such a disgraceful escapade so easily."

Belle threw her arms around Lucinda. "Pray don't be angry with me, there's a dear. Lady Grantham has already raked me down most severely and Mr. Devereux gave me the most tremendous scold on the way home.''

''None of it seems to have done the least good.''

''Oh, it has, it has. And you must know, Cinda, that I had already been punished most thoroughly. For despite what I thought, and what Mr. Stratton said, it was the most boring place. All anyone did was sit and play cards! No one paid the slightest heed to me at all. And nothing scandalous was going on. Why, Mama might have accompanied me and not been shocked. The whole thing was just a take-in!''

Lucinda laughed at her friend's air of righteous indignation. It was impossible to remain angry with Belle. ''And Mr. Stratton was not an attentive companion?''

''What! Has Mr. Devereux been tattling on me?''

''He merely mentioned Mr. Stratton's interest in cards.''

''Interest? Passion, more likely! And,'' Belle went on in the same injured tone, ''I had thought it would be so exotic, for gentlemen go there all the time and one would think it was something quite out of the usual. But it wasn't. Not a sign of an opera-dancer anywhere. It was dull and even rather sordid. I think,'' she concluded profoundly, ''that gentlemen have the oddest tastes.''

''Yes,'' Lucinda agreed sadly. She was thinking that at least two men seemed to find Chloris dePoer irresistible, and even if she were a lady, Chloris was behaving more like one of Belle's opera-dancers.

"But, Lucinda, it was so clever of you to send Mr. Devereux. It was the greatest thing. He brought his phaeton, too, and we had such a ride. How came you to think of him of all people?"

"I was at my wits' end," Lucinda confessed. "You are aware that Lady Grantham was away and Will and Sir Charles were at their sport. And I hope," she added astringently, "that you don't think I should have told my cousin and sent her to fetch you back?"

Belle giggled. "Can you imagine Mrs. Cleeson at Lucy Caldeane's?" But she won no answering smile from her friend. "Are you quite sure you're well, Cinda? You are so pale now and you seem distraught. Shall I send Will or Mrs. Cleeson to you?"

"Will? No, no thank you. I shall be better directly."

Covertly, Belle studied her friend. She had been pleased to see Mr. Devereux earlier that evening, but surprised, too. She understood that Will, Lady Grantham and Charles were away. She utterly agreed that Mrs. Cleeson could not have been involved. But why, out of all their acquaintance, had Lucinda called on Beau Devereux?

In fact, now she came to consider, the impropriety of upsetting Miss Neville had figured largely in Mr. Devereux's lecture. *I wonder,* Miss Ryland said to herself, *I very much wonder.* "I had no idea," she said aloud in elaborately casual tones, "that you and Beau Devereux were such friends."

Lucinda flushed painfully. "We are not, indeed. How can you think so? I have already explained how I came to call upon him."

"Yes, yes," Belle said soothingly, hiding her satisfaction. "I see exactly how you were placed."

"I should hope so," Lucinda declared hotly. "Mr. Devereux was most obliging. He is the kindest person and I hope you do not mean to cast aspersions on so good-hearted a response."

"Oh, I shall not, Lucinda, I assure you. I know exactly how to interpret his actions."

"Good." Lucinda stood up. "And now I think we had better return to the others."

"Yes," agreed Belle rather absently. She followed Lucinda but fell behind a little, an unaccustomed furrow in her smooth forehead. Into her huge blue eyes there crept a look, a look her friends and family had learned to mistrust: Belle Ryland was thinking.

CHAPTER THIRTEEN

NEXT MORNING, Mr. Devereux rose early and less than rested. He curtly refused all suggestions of breakfast, except for a tankard of ale, which he rapidly tossed off. Now he was dressing, but the process was not proceeding in its usual unharried way.

He stood, glowering, before the mirror in his dressing-room. On the floor beside him lay a growing pile of creased neckcloths. Impassively, Dowsett handed him another.

"And you need not," Mr. Devereux said quite unfairly, "scowl at me like that, Dowsett. A man on his way to propose is entitled to a little nervousness."

The valet's expression did not change. Not by the faintest flicker of an eyelid did Dowsett betray his interest in that pretty little trinket leaning against the studbox. "R and C" it said, didn't it?

With a muttered imprecation, Richard flung away another spoiled cravat. "It is an important decision, after all," he said through gritted teeth. "The French look upon these things more correctly. We are too romantical, too apt to be carried away by our emotions."

Stolidly, the valet passed over another rectangle of starched muslin.

"Yes, we should look at marriage more rationally, as an alliance of families, and not clutter up matters with nonsense about love. I, after all, have firsthand experience of how easily such illusions vanish." He made the final knot and stood back, frowning at himself in the looking-glass. "It will suffice," he said shortly.

Dowsett reached for the waistcoat.

"It cannot be doubted," Dev went on rather emphatically, "that Lady Chloris will always conduct herself with propriety and discretion. A man must be exceptionally finicking in his demands not to be pleased with her."

In silence Dowsett began to ease him into his coat.

"I'm glad you agree." The Beau picked up his lemon-coloured gloves and his Malacca cane. "It is, after all, more than time that the whole affair was settled."

Dowsett watched him stride downstairs and heard the front door bang behind him. He came back into the room and stared intently at the twinkling brooch and then at the rejected neckcloths. "Argh," said Dowsett thoughtfully. "Aarrgh."

By the time he had reached Eaton Square, where the dePoers lived, Dev had somewhat regained his equanimity. He squared his shoulders and asked for Lady dePoer with a strong air of resolution. The butler, he thought as he was shown into the front saloon, had a dashed knowing look.

He had barely seated himself when the door opened and Chloris burst in. She was breathless and she leaned back against the door in a way that made Devereux raise his straight black brows. A ribbon untied here, a lace trailing there suggested that she had not quite finished dressing.

"Richard," she whispered urgently, "Richard, I must speak with you."

"Certainly," he replied, resisting the impulse to whisper also. Chloris's breast heaved and there were bright spots of colour in her cheeks. He thought she looked more attractive and vivacious than he had ever seen her. "I am at your service, Chloris."

"Mama must not know I am here," she hissed, sending his brows higher. She raised a hand and placed it over her heart. "I know why you have come!"

Her air of mystery was beginning to annoy Richard. "I should think you might, Chloris," he said with some asperity. "The whole ton must..."

"I beg that you will not."

"I beg your pardon?"

"No, no! It is I who beg, beg upon my knees that you will not offer for me."

"No, really, Chloris!" Richard grasped her hands and held her upright. "This is not a Cheltenham tragedy. You may tell me perfectly well what you mean sitting down, or standing up if we must."

Chloris looked fearfully over her shoulder. "Mama must not find me here. Promise me, Richard, that you will not offer for me."

"Certainly," said Dev promptly. "Entirely as you wish. But don't you think, Chloris, that you perhaps owe me an explanation?"

Chloris's voice dropped. "I dare not—not yet." She clasped his hands. "I shall reveal all to you— soon, I promise. But till then, believe me, dear Richard, I am forever in your debt." She squeezed his hands, gave him a look of great significance and vanished.

Richard stared at the shut door and slowly shook his head. Had the whole world gone mad?

Lady dePoer came in shortly thereafter, and inventing some flummery on which to consult her, Mr. Devereux was aware that he had once again dashed that good lady's hopes. He took his leave and came thoughtfully out into the morning sun.

To his surprise, he found he was puzzled, but not at all dismayed. In fact, as he walked on, his step was positively jaunty and his demeanour in no way suggested a man who had just been disappointed in love.

IF MR. DEVEREUX HAD FOUND his morning surprising, in Cavendish Square, Patience Grantham was finding hers equally astounding. She sat on Belle's bed, her soft brown eyes wide, and repeated, for the third time, "But, are you sure, Belle?"

Despite the early hour, that young lady was nibbling sweetmeats from a silver-paper-covered box, just delivered that morning by one of her admirers. "Of course I'm sure," she replied, her attention on the box. "I wish you will try some of this marchpane, Patience. I have not tasted any quite like it. And see how cunningly it has been shaped. Is this not the perfect likeness of a peach?''

"Never mind the marchpane," said Patience firmly. "It's just that...well, I always thought that she and Will..."

"Certainly not! Don't be such a gudgeon!"

"But if what you say is true, why should we interfere? Why don't we leave it to Lucinda and—"

"Haven't you been listening to what I've been telling you? We can't possibly do that."

"Why not?" asked Patience reasonably.

Less intrepid conspirators than Miss Ryland might have described this as a leveller, but Belle was not at a loss for long. "Pride," she asserted triumphantly, her mouth full of almond paste.

"Pride?"

"Pride. You know, Patience, that we women would rather die than admit our affection, if we do not know that we are loved in return. We keep such things secret till we are sure." She bit into another sweetmeat, pleased by her own perception.

Whether she was also struck by Belle's insight, or whether by some thought of her own, Patience coloured a little and looked away.

"So, you see, that is all we are doing; giving them an opportunity to see that their feelings are wholly reciprocated. It's a noble task." Belle selected a piece of marchpane in the form of a pineapple.

"We-e-ell..." said Patience doubtfully.

"Patience! You are not going to be an addle-plot, are you?"

"I just do not see how telling Lucinda a great number of lies is going to make her any happier."

Belle swallowed indignantly. "I never imagined you could be so prosy. They're not precisely lies, just a way of setting the scene. Don't you care what happens to Lucinda, or Will for that matter?"

"Of course I care! But how does this plan of yours..."

"Haven't you heard the on-dits? Everyone expects a betrothal. Lady Borely practically held on to me, demanding to be told the wedding date. But if Lucinda cares for someone else, how happy could Will be in such an engagement?"

"Not, not at all," Patience said in a constricted voice. "That would be dreadful."

"Then remember we're doing this to bring Lucinda and Mr. Devereux together and also to save my brother from a loveless marriage."

"But Belle, if Lucinda does not love Will, why would..." She faltered at Belle's furious glance. "Oh, very well. I shall try to do as you say, though I don't think I shall make a very convincing actress."

"You will manage. Just remember that you must make her believe that you are quite distraught."

"I shall be that indeed," said Patience dryly.

"She must realize that it is imperative for you to make such a trip." Reluctantly Belle replaced the lid of the sweetmeat box, now much depleted. "You'd better go and get ready. Lucinda will need time to arrange to be free tonight."

"What are you going to do?"

"I," said Belle grandly, "must consider my strategy—and my disguise."

"Are you sure Lucinda won't recognize you?"

"I shall wear a hat and a mask, and anyhow, she won't be expecting to see me there."

"That's true, but do you not think she might be unduly frightened, accosted in the dark while she is alone?"

"She will be rescued directly and I shall run off just as soon as he arrives."

Patience frowned. "There are so many things that could go wrong. To get the timing right..."

Belle sighed. "Patience, are you trying to throw a damp on me? Just make sure that you get Lucinda there. I shall take care of everything else."

"I wish I could be sure that this is the right thing to do."

Again Belle sighed dramatically, but Patience just shook her head and took her leave without another word.

Miss Ryland's next proceedings were remarkable, to say the least. Very quietly, she opened her bedroom door and peered up and down the hall. Then she ran lightly over to Will's door. She let herself in and went straight to the big carved wardrobe.

She rifled through the garments hanging there, till she came upon a long black travelling cloak with a hood attached. She tossed it onto the bed. Then she chose a pair of black Hessians with spotless white tops. She sighed as she put them by the cloak. She would have to stuff the toes with tissue, for they were far too large.

Finally, she took a shirt and a dark, swallow-tailed coat and breeches. Wrapping everything in the cloak, Belle stole back to her own room. Pleased not to have been seen, she stowed her bundle on the dusty top of her wardrobe. After washing her hands she went downstairs.

In Sir Charles's study, she seated herself at his huge oak desk. She tugged open drawers till she found his supply of writing paper. From the sheets, she chose only those without a crest; then she picked up the long quill-pen.

She chewed meditatively on the end and then began to write. But the result did not please her. She tossed the sheet into the waste-paper basket and began again. She had scrunched up several sheets before she was satisfied with the wording.

After rereading it, she dropped a few more blots of ink over the criss-crossed page. She searched through her host's seals, and after finding a plain one, she put the letter in an envelope and stamped the wet wax.

Next, she scrawled the address and again decorated it with more artistically placed blots and smudges. Finally she rang for a footman and handed over the letter.

Smiling to herself, Belle went back upstairs. During the morning and afternoon, she behaved with such charming agreeableness that Lady Grantham was moved to describe her as "a very prettily behaved child, after all."

"But you, Patience," she said, turning to her daughter, "you have been so quiet. Are you not well?"

"She looks very pale," Belle put in solicitously.

"She does, she does." Lady Grantham looked worried. "Perhaps we have been overdoing it of late."

"She looks exhausted," Belle intoned so sepulchrally that Patience responded indignantly.

"Don't talk about me as if I were burnt to the socket!"

"Nevertheless," said her mother, "it may be as well if we have a restful evening for a change. There is only Mrs. Manley-Smythe's rout and that is always such a dreadful squeeze that we shall not be missed. Yes, the more I think of it, the more I consider we shall do well to be quiet tonight."

"And you will be able to visit your aunt again, Godmama."

"You are a thoughtful girl, Belle. Though, truth to tell, Dorcas is like to outlive us all. But I shall take your suggestion. I may be easy in mind if you girls are safe at home."

"We shall be safe and cosy," Belle assured her, but behind her ladyship's back, she risked a wink at Patience.

But Miss Grantham only sighed and shook her head. She had not enjoyed her interview with Lucinda, and even now, she could scarcely repress a shudder as she remembered that harrowing morning visit . . .

"Mrs. Cleeson will not be anxious if you say you are coming to us this evening, will she?" Patience had faltered, unable to meet Lucinda's wondering eyes.

"No, naturally not." Lucinda had looked closely at the other girl. Patience was clearly distraught, staring miserably at the carpet and picking constantly at the fringe of her reticule. "But is this secrecy really necessary? Cannot you tell me a little more about why we must go to Vauxhall Gardens tonight and why we must tell no one?"

"No, no I can't!" Patience looked as though she might burst into tears. How she wished she had never agreed to Belle's hare-brained scheme. But she had promised to do her best and there was . . . well, there was that other matter . . .

Patience squared her shoulders. "Just say you'll come with me, Lucinda." Her voice quavered. "I don't know what I shall do if you refuse me."

Touched, Lucinda patted her hand. "There, Patience, I didn't mean to pry. Of course I shall go with you and help you if I can."

Patience looked even more wretched. "Oh, dear, I don't know . . . Perhaps I shouldn't . . . Oh, what is the best thing to do!"

"Don't worry," Lucinda said as hearteningly as she could. "Whatever your reasons, I am sure they are excellent ones. I shall come to you this evening and we shall go to Vauxhall together."

When she left a few minutes later, Patience was still upset and not apparently calmed by her friend's promise. Lucinda watched her departure, frowning slightly. What could it all mean?

She was in truth a little shocked to find Patience proposing that they make such an expedition without chaperons and without telling anyone. If it were Belle, now, she would be suspicious. But Patience? It was impossible to imagine her doing anything disreputable. It must be a matter of the greatest urgency to persuade her to act with such disregard for propriety.

She went thoughtfully to find Mrs. Cleeson, who was trying on a rather dashing bonnet with blue silk roses.

"Ah, there you are, Lucinda. Be sure you take a wide-brimmed hat with you, as you will be looking up into the sun. You must not get freckles—especially since your ball is less than a week away."

Lucinda stared at her cousin. "Are we going out, then?"

"Gracious heaven, child!" Mrs. Cleeson secured the hat with a large, pearl-topped pin. "It was your idea entirely. For you know I saw Lunardi's first flight when I was younger than you and I do not think anything could equal the excitement of that."

"Oh! The balloon ascent!" Lucinda said listlessly.

"If you've changed your mind, we need not go."

"No, we might as well do that as anything. I shall fetch my hat."

As Lucinda trailed off, Mrs. Cleeson gazed, astonished, after her.

It was another beautiful day with bright sun in a cloudless blue sky. Ideal for ballooning, Mrs. Cleeson had said knowledgeably.

Lucinda forced herself to look interested. After all, Mrs. Cleeson was right. She had pestered her duenna to view the balloon ascent. But that, she thought, sighing, had been before her promise to Patience. Now, apprehension about the coming evening had spoiled her enjoyment of the outing.

They had almost reached Moorfields when the carriage lurched suddenly, throwing Lucinda and Mrs. Cleeson into each other. As they struggled to sort themselves out, the coach came to a stop, tilting rather precariously to one side.

John Coachman rushed to open one door. "How be you, ladies?"

"We are unhurt, but what has happened?" Mrs. Cleeson clung to a strap with one hand and tried to right her hat with the other.

"It's the axle, mum, cracked or I'm a dutch-man."

"Cracked! That sounds serious."

"So it be. We'll have to get someone to help us to a wheelwright."

Gingerly, Mrs. Cleeson leaned out of the open door and looked about. "Ah, we are within walking distance of the Artillery Grounds. Do you, coachman, do whatever you can. Miss Neville and I shall take a hackney back."

With the help of the coachman, Lucinda and her cousin descended from the disabled coach. They began to walk towards the grounds of the Honourable Artillery Company.

Almost immediately Lucinda was aware of the countrified atmosphere, so different from that of the crowded city. The houses were farther apart, with carefully tended gardens. Laundresses were laying snowy washing on the open green and she actually saw one small boy leading a goat out to pasture.

At any other time, Lucinda's spirits would have risen, but now she regarded these sights with a lack-lustre eye.

"There will be rather a crowd," Mrs. Cleeson observed. "Many of them on foot like ourselves."

There was indeed a considerable number of persons, all of them gaily dressed and in a holiday mood, moving in the same direction.

Once inside the grounds, Lucinda and cousin Ethelreda found a place in the circle about the balloon. Lucinda stared at it.

A number of men milled about what looked like an enormous basket, tethered by ropes, and seemingly built on a kind of platform. From there, some odd-looking cylinders protruded. Two men seemed to be filling them with something.

"Hydrogen," Mrs. Cleeson told her. "They must be very careful with it."

But most intriguing of all was what appeared to be a creased bundle of red, white and blue silk lying behind the basket, but attached to it by long, bright yellow cords.

"It will be very beautiful when inflated," Ethelreda said. "The silk is oiled, you know." She smiled reminiscently. "How I remember how we cheered when Lunardi lifted off. And what a handsome young man he was. I vow I dreamed about him for days afterwards."

Lucinda didn't think anyone would be dreaming about the present balloonist. He was a plump little man, with gold-rimmed spectacles. He was striding up and down in front of the balloon, pausing to confer with one of the workmen or to nod self-importantly at one of the crowd.

There seemed to be a hiatus in the preparations, so Lucinda took a closer look at the crowd. She saw a few slight acquaintances, but not many members of the haut ton.

"Ballooning has become quite an everyday thing now," said Ethelreda, who was also scanning the crowd, "so people have rather tended to become blasé about it." She waved her fan gently, then suddenly snapped it shut. "There! Was that not Belle's maid—Mabel, is it not?"

Lucinda followed her gesture. But the crowd, restless at the delay, was constantly shifting. "I can see nothing of her, cousin."

"I suppose there is no reason why Mabel should not attend an entertainment. Belle must have give her a holiday."

Lucinda nodded, but she kept her eyes on the same spot. Mabel might be on holiday, but then again . . .

"Look! They are going to ignite the fuel."

The crowd shifted in anticipation, and just for a second, Lucinda saw Belle. She was laughing, her head tilted flirtatiously towards the unmistakable figure of Miles Stratton. Stratton bent to speak to her and they were hidden from Lucinda again.

There was a sudden sharp bang and when she looked at the balloon again, the silk had begun to rise. Slowly it unfolded itself, stretched into a great curve and hung above the basket. Lucinda saw that it, too, was now floating, held to earth only by four thick ropes.

The plump gentleman stood in the gondola, his pocket watch in his hand, the other raised. The hand fell; there was a shout, the crack of a pistol and four men sprang forward and cut the cords.

The crowd shouted wildly and many waved their hats. The balloon rose straight in the air. For a moment it hung there like some great, brilliantly coloured bird. Then it took the air currents and began to move more quickly, climbing higher in an easterly direction.

For a moment, Lucinda's heart rose with it. Then her troubles came rushing back upon her. She sighed and turned to her cousin.

"So lovely," murmured Mrs. Cleeson, still gazing after the rapidly diminishing balloon. "I declare it quite makes one want to venture up oneself."

"I completely agree with you, Mrs. Cleeson. But what says Miss Neville?"

Lucinda swung round and found herself staring at Beau Devereux. She dropped her eyes in immediate confusion.

"Well, Miss Neville?" he repeated in a rallying tone. "Do you share your cousin's ambition to be a balloonist?"

Lucinda peeped up at him under her long lashes. Well, if he could greet her in such a manner after their last encounter, then she, too, could master her feelings. She lifted her chin. "Why, yes, sir," she said with admirable composure, "I believe I should like to essay such a mode of travel."

She glanced up at the now tiny black speck in the sky. A note of wistfulness entered her voice. "It must be wonderful to rise above the earth like that, to leave all one's cares behind one..."

Dev looked quickly down at her, but before he could speak, cousin Ethelreda clasped a hand to her forehead.

"Speaking of cares—I had quite forgotten our coach problem. We must hurry if we are to get a hackney in this crowd." She turned to Dev. "I wonder if I may trespass upon your kindness, Mr. Devereux. Our carriage sustained a breakdown on our journey here and I wonder if I might prevail upon you to call a cab for us."

"I'll do more than that," he replied promptly. "I came in my own curricle and I should be more than pleased to drive you home."

"Why, that would be most obliging in you. We shall be most grateful, shall we not, Lucinda?" Mrs. Cleeson nudged her charge encouragingly.

"Oh! Oh, yes! Of course! Most grateful," Lucinda stuttered. But her heart sank at the thought of a long journey with that very disturbing gentleman.

Dev's tiger had been looking after the horses at a nearby inn. When he saw Mr. Devereux, he handed him the ribbons with a cheery salute and hopped up onto a perch at the rear of the vehicle.

"Will you sit beside me while I drive, Miss Neville? These chestnuts are not the equal of our Castor and Pollux, but I think they have their points nonetheless."

"Yes, do, Lucinda. I shall be glad to have some time to go over my lists again. What with the ball and other things, there seems so much to do these past few days."

Giving her cousin a dark look, Lucinda reluctantly climbed up front.

For a while, Mr. Devereux was occupied in threading a way through the pedestrians and other vehicles. But when the traffic was moving smoothly he turned to Lucinda.

"So your ball is to be in three days, Miss Neville? You must be quite excited about that."

"Yes," said Lucinda hollowly. Then, feeling that this sounded rather bald, she added, "Very."

Dev gave his attention to the road again. There was silence. As though he had just made up his mind, he said suddenly, "Miss Neville, I have been wanting an opportunity to speak with you since—"

"Oh, hush, sir! I pray you, hush!" She cast an agonized glance behind her, but Mrs. Cleeson was murmuring happily over her lists.

"That brooch—I must explain to you—"

"No! No!" Lucinda held up an arm as though to ward off a blow. She could not bear to hear Mr. Devereux declare his love for Chloris, to hear his voice soften with affection as he spoke of the love-token—the very token Chloris had so carelessly discarded. If his love was untrue, he would not hear it from her. "I beg you, sir," she said in a choked voice, "to let it be. You owe me no explanation whatsoever. Pray believe that I have no desire to meddle in your private affairs. Let us say no more of this."

Dev was silent for a few moments. Then his shoulders lifted slightly and he shook the reins. "As you wish, Miss Neville," he said in a colourless voice. "Let us talk of the balloon ascent."

"Are you—" Lucinda swallowed and with a great effort mastered her own tones "—are you much interested in such matters?"

"I was much interested in this one, for there were certain modifications in the balloon's design that I wished to observe in action. If you noticed the hydrogen containers, you will have observed that they..."

Miserably, Lucinda listened as his voice ran on, explaining weights and wind drift and other such technical matters. The sun was at its afternoon height, but she felt cold.

She ran her hands over her bare arms and tried to concentrate on what he was saying. She made the appropriate responses, but ever afterwards she could not remember what she had said.

But at last the nightmarish journey ended. Richard handed down both his passengers, but refused Mrs. Cleeson's offer of refreshment. He took his leave in a punctilious but utterly impersonal manner.

In a black cloud of despair, Lucinda followed her cousin into the house.

CHAPTER FOURTEEN

ONCE SHE WAS BACK in Agincourt Circle, all Lucinda's apprehensions about the evening flooded back. As a last resort, she found herself hoping rather chicken-heartedly that Mrs. Cleeson would throw a rub in their way by insisting that she carry out their evening engagements.

But when she had left off her hat, freshened her toilette and gone in search of her cousin, she found that good lady prostrate on her bed.

"Are you not well, cousin?" she asked in concern.

Mrs. Cleeson moaned and removed a cloth reeking of rose-water from her forehead. "I knew this would happen. Exactly the same thing came about when I went to see Lunardi."

"You have the megrim, cousin Ethelreda?"

"From staring into the sun." With a sigh, Mrs. Cleeson replaced the damp cloth.

Tentatively, Lucinda broached the subject dominating her thoughts. "If you shouldn't mind too much, cousin, Lady Grantham must visit her aunt again and Patience has asked me to bear them company tonight..."

"What an excellent idea! Do go and visit Patience and Belle tonight. I don't doubt Amelia is anxious to miss the rout. Mrs. Manley-Smythe's parties are always a perfect crush. I own I shall also be glad to avoid this one."

Lucinda said nothing, merely gazed ahead of her, her fingers twisting and untwisting in Ethelreda's counterpane.

Mrs. Cleeson looked thoughtfully at her. "Is Will to be at home tonight?" she asked casually.

"No." Lucinda's mind was on the night's excursion. "I believe not."

"Ah." Mrs. Cleeson nodded and thought to herself that his absence probably accounted for her charge's mopes. She made an effort to speak cheerfully. "Gentlemen cannot be forever dangling after us, you know," she said. "They have their own interests."

Dispiritedly, Lucinda agreed, and left her cousin to the quiet of her darkened room. Time, however, marched relentlessly forward. Having dawdled as long as she dared over dinner, Lucinda went upstairs with a feeling of impending doom.

Mindful of Patience's instructions, she chose a dark-coloured wrap with a hood. The Grantham coach called for her, and feeling rather as she imagined Marie Antoinette must have done when she entered the tumbril for the guillotine, Lucinda climbed the steps. To her surprise she found Patience, similarly garbed, already inside.

"Are we going already, then?"

"I thought it would be best," replied Patience in a rush, not meeting Lucinda's eyes.

Out of respect for her friend's privacy, Lucinda did not ask any further questions. But she couldn't help thinking that Belle would have been a far more daring and courageous companion for such an adventure. She herself was increasingly uneasy, and she hoped desperately that they would not meet anyone they knew.

Last time she had come to Vauxhall, in a large and properly chaperoned party, they had arrived by Vauxhall Stairs and the river. But this time, they entered by the far less imposing land gate.

Hoods pulled forward and cloaks clutched tightly about them, the girls hurried forward. There were already a number of merry-makers present. The lights twinkled in the growing dark; the fountains played; music from the bandstands floated on the night air and laughter rose and fell around them.

But the girls paid no attention to Vauxhall's many attractions. Lucinda was in fact cheered to see that Patience knew where she was going and was avoiding the brightly lit areas as much as possible. Dodging the crowd, they crossed to where the promenades and more secluded walks began.

It was quieter and darker there. Lucinda began to feel there was something to be said for the lights, after all. She looked longingly back, but Patience propelled her down one of the side walks.

"The second, yes, here we are." She pulled Lucinda after her. "Ah, here it is." She indicated a kind of archway cut out of the thick hedge that bordered the walk on both sides. There was a small wrought-iron bench in the alcove which had been so formed.

"Wait here, Lucinda," Patience said abruptly and turned and fled.

"Patience! Wait, Patience!" But Miss Grantham had vanished into night and Lucinda was alone.

She fell back on the bench. Huddling closer to the corner, she pulled her wrap nearer and glanced nervously from side to side. Where had Patience gone? When would she be back? What would happen to her, all alone in this dreadful place?

She wished desperately she had never agreed to come at all. Even the most crowded rout would be preferable to this!

On the other side of the hedge, pressed back against the branches, Patience was wishing exactly the same thing. Anxiously, she peered along the path. Where was Belle? Surely it was time for Belle to make her appearance? Patience groped for her watch. Yes! Past time. How much longer must they wait? What was Belle *doing*?

On the other side of the gardens, behind the Chinese Pavilion, Belle was experiencing unforeseen difficulties.

"Oh, miss," exclaimed a rather frightened Mabel. "Perhaps you didn't ought to wear the cloak. It's so long, it does trip you up."

Belle hitched the garment higher on her shoulders. "It's not the cloak," she complained. "It's this mask. Either it slips down or, if I pull it tight, I can't see properly."

Mabel glanced fearfully about. There were few people here and the shadows lay thickly about them. "Maybe I should go with you, miss."

"No, Mabel. I can't go accosting young women with a maid in attendance. No, you stay here with my clothes. I shall need you to help me change. After all, I can't go home dressed like this."

Mabel looked unhappy and sniffed disconsolately.

"Just stay here, at the back of the Pavilion. No one will see you and I shall know exactly where to find you. Don't worry, everything is going splendidly."

Even Belle's confidence, however, faltered a little when she found herself caught up in the press of people in front of the private boxes. The mask restricted her vision, especially on the side. The cloak hung heavily on her and displayed an aggravating tendency to catch her up. And the boots! They were the worst of all. To get anywhere, she had to adopt a most peculiar sliding shuffle. "Really," muttered Belle to herself, "I can't think how men manage at all!"

Most peculiar indeed, thought Mr. Devereux as he stood by the classical ruins, watching the crowd. He was not at the moment referring to Belle's gait. Rather he was considering the letter he had received that morning. His finger tapped against the pocket where he had stowed it.

Expensive notepaper...illiterate spelling. Well-formed writing...yet covered in blots. Unsigned...yet delivered by a uniformed footman. If only the maid who received it had recognized the livery!

And the reference to Miss Neville: what could that mean and how could she require his help? Dev shook his head. There was a havycavy air to the whole business. He was probably making a prize cake of himself.

"At ten o'clock," it had said. It must be getting close on ten now. The second promenade, wasn't it, and the first alcove? Just as likely he'd find only a moon-struck couple there—and much they'd thank him for intruding!

Mr. Devereux eyed the lively crowd with disfavour. He'd never greatly cared for Vauxhall; not good ton, not at all.

"Good Lord, Dev! What on earth are you doing here? I thought you loathed the place."

Dev swung round to greet Captain Rupert Brookefield, one of his closest friends. "Rupert! I thought you were in Belgium."

"Just got back, my dear boy. Enjoying a long-delayed and, may I say, well-deserved furlough. But I hear I am to wish you happy?"

"I beg your pardon?"

"Don't be coy, my boy. The fair Chloris. I hear she is soon to become Mrs. Devereux."

"I congratulate you, Rupert. If you've just got back, you seem remarkably well informed on the latest gossip. But this particular on-dit is wrong. I am not going to marry Lady Chloris.''

"You're not? If that don't beat all! I bet Farquhar at White's this morning that you'd be married before the Season's out.''

Mr. Devereux regarded his friend, his smile carving his lips and warming his eyes. "Did you indeed? Well, don't despair. You may yet win your wager.''

"Oho! Now what's to—'' Captain Brookefield broke off and raised his monocle. "Look at that over there, Dev. Demme if I don't think you're right. Vauxhall ain't the thing. You know, I breakfasted with young Bertram this morning and for a moment I thought he was wearing an army tent instead of breeches. Now there's another sprig in the same rig-out.''

"I take it the Petersham trousers do not meet with your approval?''

"They do not! I tell you, Dev, I don't know what the younger generation's coming to. Take that young chap over there, now.'' He pointed to a young man crossing the grassy square in front of them.

"I shouldn't care to patronize his bootmaker,'' Richard agreed.

"And that cloak—he might be goin' to a costume ball. I shouldn't wonder he's wearing a mask—I should myself if I went about got up like that. Tell you what it is, Ricky, the country's gone to the dogs since I left.''

Dev laughed, but his gaze followed that absurd figure. Surely there was something familiar about…

A raucous group of revellers suddenly caught up with the object of their interest, singing boisterously and linking arms as they dragged him along with them.

"I'm desolate to have to leave you, Rupert, but I have an appointment."

"A mysterious assignation, eh? Who is she, my boy?"

"Come and dine tomorrow. I cannot stay now."

"I certainly shall. Off you go now, my boy. After all, I must protect my bet."

Dev grasped his friend's hand and set off for the rendezvous.

If Mr. Devereux was less than enthusiastic about Vauxhall, there was one visitor that evening who took an even more jaundiced view of the amusement park. Unexpectedly released from the duties of escorting either his sister or Miss Neville, Will Ryland had accepted a friend's invitation and joined a party bound for Vauxhall. Once there, however, he had discovered he was not at all in the mood for frivolity.

Absorbed in his own reflections, he had wandered away from the crowds. But an hour of walking and thinking had brought him no solace and he was now seeking to rejoin his companions. He had spent a tedious half hour wandering byways and dark paths and upsetting a surprising number of courting couples.

Now, however, he could see brighter lights and catch snatches of music. That must be the main promenade at last, he thought, hastening his steps. He would take leave of his friends and go home.

Then he froze. He had heard a scream, a woman's scream. Mr. Ryland raced down the lane towards the sound.

"No, no!" Lucinda cried, pushing the man back.

"What is a pretty li'l ladybird like you doin' all alone, eh? That's what I'd like to know." The fellow leered at her, bringing his red face close to hers and choking her with his brandy-soaked breath. "Poor li'l ladybird," he hiccupped.

Lucinda slipped off the bench and backed away. Where was Patience?

"Naughty, naughty!" The red-faced man attempted to wag a finger at her and stumbled forward.

Lucinda backed away again, but he lurched towards her and grasped her round the waist.

"Let me go! Let me go!" Lucinda struggled, half in anger, half in fear.

"You heard the lady," said a grim voice.

"Will!" gasped Lucinda.

"No fair," declared the red-faced man, pulling Lucinda closer. "No fair, I saw the li'l ladybird first."

Will drew back one arm, and with a powerful crack, his fist contacted the red-faced man's chin. Lucinda's tormentor sank silently to the ground.

Miss Grantham, Miss Ryland and Mr. Richard Devereux turned the corner just in time to hear Lucinda cry, "Will, thank heavens!" and to see her throw her arms about his neck before sinking into a dead faint in Mr. Ryland's arms.

CHAPTER FIFTEEN

EARLY NEXT MORNING, Will made his way quietly down to the library in Cavendish Square. He stood before the fireplace, kicking the brass fender and moodily staring at the pair of crossed swords over the mantelpiece. His face was clouded and his shoulders drooped.

"Will!" The soft voice broke his reverie.

"Patience! I hardly dared to hope...after last night..."

"Hush, Will." Patience drew him down beside her on the sofa, but he was not comforted.

"I have no right to ask anything of you, no right at all."

"No right?" Patience asked almost inaudibly. "No right, Will?"

Will uttered a sound halfway between a moan and a groan. He drove his fingers through his blond curls. "But don't you see? That only makes it worse. As long as I thought I was the only one...but now I know that you must suffer, too, how much more difficult it is to bear that!"

Patience said, "You are sure there is no hope? No possibility that there is, well, someone else?"

Will's fingers tore at his hair. "I wish there were. But you saw how it was last night. You saw how she threw herself into my arms."

A tear trickled down Patience's cheek. "Yes," she choked out, "I saw."

"And I have told you how generously she behaved, how loyally, thinking only how to help me and my family. It is due entirely to her father's efforts that we have come even this far out of dun territory. I shudder to think what would have happened if the Nevilles had not come to our aid. How despicable it would be in me to cast her off now."

"No, no, of course you cannot do anything of the sort."

Will passed a hand over his brow. "That is why I dared to ask for this meeting—" his voice trembled "—this last meeting."

Patience sobbed convulsively. Will leaned towards her. She raised her tear-drenched face to his. In a moment he gathered her to him and kissed her despairingly.

"Aha!" Sir Charles Grantham flung the library door wide and stood glaring at his sister and Will.

Sir Charles was not in the best of tempers and he had been prowling the house since early morning, looking for an opportunity to vent his anger and frustration.

The previous night he had looked forward to a cosy evening at home with Belle and had refused Will's invitation to Vauxhall, only to be informed by his butler that Belle was spending the evening with

Miss Neville. Sir Charles had prepared an elaborately casual reason for calling on the Nevilles, only
to be obliged to endure a long chat with Mrs. Cleeson, who commiserated with him on not going home
first and finding Lucinda spending the evening at his
own house. Sir Charles had not given Belle away to
Mrs. Cleeson, but he was seething with rage when he
finally escaped.

He had a strong suspicion that Belle was up to one
of her tricks again, but he could find no trace of her
at any of the tonnish engagements he had dropped in
upon; nor to his chagrin, had he seen Miles Stratton. He had gone home in the worst temper ever and
spent an endless evening pacing his study and planning ways to bring Belle to a full realization of her
iniquity.

That mood had not improved when Belle and Patience at last appeared. Belle had been clearly upset:
she had dashed past him, refusing to speak. She had
been dressed in the most extraordinary fashion, too.
Sir Charles could not be sure, but he *thought* he had
actually glimpsed breeches beneath that ridiculous
cape.

Baulked of his prey in Belle, Charles had cor-
nered his sister and demanded she explain. But Patience had been uncharacteristically terse, saying only
that they had been hearing about Will Ryland's engagement to Miss Neville, before she too fled upstairs.

And now, here was Ryland embracing her in the
library, the very morning after he had become en-

gaged to someone else. Sir Charles's desire for a scene had been thwarted last night; now he perceived that he had a glorious opportunity.

"Aha!" he repeated, pleased with the menacing tone he had achieved. The effect on the others was no less pleasing. The guilty pair whirled round and jumped apart.

"Charles!" gasped Patience.

"Well might you stare, my girl!" Sir Charles was getting into his stride. "I wonder you dare look me in the face."

"Now, see here, Grantham—"

"No, you see here, Ryland. Are you or are you not engaged to Lucinda Neville?"

Will exchanged glances with Patience. "Well..." he began.

"Well me no wells," commanded Sir Charles, his hand raised in a haughty gesture of rejection. "Yes or no?"

Will looked again at Patience. "Yes," he admitted slowly.

"And I find you making love to my sister! By God!" Charles remembered a line from the last play he'd seen and happily made use of it. "By God, sir, you'll answer to me for this."

Patience grasped at the edge of the desk. "Wh-what do you mean?" she faltered.

"This!" Sir Charles vaulted onto a fireside chair and reached for the swords over the mantelpiece.

"Grantham," Will cried, gaping at him, "you can't be serious!"

"Can I not?" Sir Charles leapt to the floor. "This, sir—" he presented the hilt of the sword to Will "—is a matter of honour."

"Hono- No, dash it all, Grantham, your sister's honour is perfectly untouched. I hold her in the greatest esteem, I—"

"You do, do you?"

"Yes, yes, Charles, he has never—"

"Madam," said Sir Charles, making a sweeping gesture with the sword and beheading several of the roses in a silver bowl on the side table. "Madam, this is no matter for females."

"It's no matter for swords," said Will. "Good God, Grantham, do you think I'm going to fight a duel with you in your own library, with your sister present?"

"So," sneered Sir Charles, availing himself of yet another line from the performance, "so you are a coward as well as a rake?"

Will flushed. "Just who are you calling a coward?"

Sir Charles smiled loftily and held out the sword.

Will grasped it. "I'll not take that from you or anyone else."

"Will," cried Patience, "you cannot be so foolish!"

But Will had begun the salute with Charles. With a snap he brought the sword down and the two of them sprang into the en garde position.

Both young gentlemen had been expensively tutored in the art of the *duello*. But it is doubtful if either of their erstwhile masters would have been gratified by his pupil's present performance. They lurched and lumbered about, lunging vainly at each other and dodging pieces of furniture.

Her knuckles pressed to her lips, Patience watched them, and even to her inexperienced eyes, it began to appear that they were not in immediate danger of killing each other.

"Grantham," Will panted, edging behind an armchair, "hadn't we better call this whole thing off?"

"Damn you, Ryland!" Sir Charles attempted to lunge around a huge Chinese vase. "Stand still and fight!"

That, of course, was the last thing Will intended doing. Standing away from the vase, he let Charles's attack fall short. Then he hopped nimbly behind the sofa.

With a roar, Charles raced after him. Raising his sword, he aimed straight for Will's chest, but instead stumbled over a rug and plunged his blade deep into the sofa cushions. A cloud of white feathers instantly enveloped his head.

"Really, my dear fellow—" Beau Devereux walked around the transfixed Patience and lifted his monocle "—if you don't care for the colour, surely it would be tidier to send for the upholsterer?"

"Dash it, Dev, what are you doing here?"

"I came to see if you had all recovered from the events of last night. But I perceive," he remarked, as he watched Charles tug his sword out, releasing another gush of feathers, "that your energies are quite unimpaired."

"What on earth are you doing with all those feathers?" It was Belle, who was now gazing into the room. She wore a pelisse and gloves, as though she had just come in. "Have I been missing all the fun?"

"Fun!" Sir Charles resumed his role. "Your brother, madam, has been making love to my sister, if you call that fun."

"Will and Patience?" Belle looked from one to the other. "*Now* I see."

Mr. Devereux was not at all sure that he did, but he too stared thoughtfully at Will and Patience.

Will flushed under all this scrutiny. "I was not making love to Miss Grantham," he said with dignity. "I was saying goodbye to her."

"Goodbye?" echoed Charles and Belle in unison. Dev said nothing, but his expression of interest deepened.

Patience sank down on the sofa, causing another eruption of feathers, and said, "Mr. Ryland is betrothed to Miss Neville."

"Is he indeed?" murmured Dev.

Sir Charles's attention had been increasingly focussed on Belle, who looked provokingly fresh and carefree. Regarding her, he felt his grievances of the night before return in full. "Miss Ryland," he ground out, "have the goodness to retire to the back salon with me. There are certain matters I wish to discuss with you."

At the moment, however, Belle was concentrating on her brother. "Do you mean to say," she said, as though trying to understand some abstruse philosophical point, "that you don't wish to be engaged to Lucinda, and that it is Patience you prefer?"

"I shall not discuss either Miss Grantham or Miss Neville," said Will stiffly. He did not look at Patience, who sat twisting her handkerchief and gazing at the floor.

"Very proper," approved Mr. Devereux. "But, do you know, I believe that you may have been somewhat beforehand in your farewells to Miss Grantham?"

Will and Patience blinked at him, but Belle began to smile. Sir Charles ignored the others and glared steadily at her.

"What...what do you mean, sir?" Patience asked tentatively, scarcely daring to hope.

"Do you mean, sir—" understanding was dawning in Will's eyes "—do you mean that Lucinda—"

"I mean that Charles should be grateful he eviscerated his mother's sofa and not his future brother-in-law."

Will and Patience turned joyfully to each other. But Sir Charles snapped, "Miss Ryland, I am waiting."

A quick glance at his face told Belle it was time to be conciliating. "I am coming, Sir Charles, pray excuse me," she murmured submissively, "but first I must deliver a message to Mr. Devereux."

Dev's eyebrows rose.

"I have just returned from Miss Neville's," she said, looking directly into his eyes. "She asked me to relay a message to you. She begs you will call in Agincourt Circle at your earliest convenience."

"How very prescient of Miss Neville to know that you would find me here. And, do you know, Miss Ryland, is it not odd that since I met you, I find the number of unusual messages I receive has increased alarmingly?"

"What can you mean, sir?" Belle returned his gaze with one of limpid incomprehension.

"Madam," said Sir Charles through gritted teeth, "I am still waiting."

As Belle passed Mr. Devereux, her guileless expression did not change, but she paused for a moment and just before she followed Charles out of the room, she closed one blue eye at Richard.

Dev picked up his cane. "Pray convey my regrets to your mother, Miss Grantham. I find I am called away."

Neither Patience nor Will paid him the slightest heed. They sat side by side on the wounded sofa, their gazes and hands locked, while feathers settled unnoticed on their hair and shoulders.

"Your servant, Miss Grantham, Ryland." The Beau executed one of his flawless bows and, brushing a few stray feathers from his coat, set out for his second call of the morning.

HE HAD GONE about halfway to his destination when he heard running feet behind him. On turning, he beheld Sidney, the youngest of his footmen, pounding towards him.

Panting, Sidney drew level with him and held out a letter.

"Thank you." Mr. Devereux took the envelope. He raised his eyebrows as he recognized the crest. "When did this arrive, Sidney?"

The footman took a deep breath. "About an hour ago, sir. Mr. Dowsett said it was important. He promised me a sovereign if I found you, sir."

"How loquacious of him." murmured Mr. Devereux, as he slit the envelope with his thumb and extracted a single sheet of heavily criss-crossed and underlined script. His brows rose higher as he read. Then, carefully and slowly, he read it again.

"Mr. Dowsett was right," he told Sidney, pocketing it. "It is a most important letter."

Sidney looked pleased. "He gave me a list of places to try, sir. Lady Grantham's was first and they told me I'd just missed you. The blond young lady told me your direction and I ran as fast as I could."

"A Trojan effort, Sidney."

"Thank you, sir." Sidney beamed. "Oh, and one other thing, Mr. Devereux. The coachman gave this to Mr. Dowsett this morning. It was found when they were cleaning the grey curricle." He retrieved another piece of paper from his pocket.

Dev took the rather crumpled sheet and glanced quickly at it. "Not my handwriting. Looks like some sort of list. Must have been dropped yesterday." He pushed it into his own pocket. "I'm obliged to you,

Sidney." He tossed a coin into the footman's hand, and with a friendly nod, continued on his way.

Sidney glanced down and then his mouth fell open. In his palm lay a bright golden guinea.

The morning, reflected Mr. Devereux, was decidedly improving. He suppressed an urge to drag his cane along the iron railings in front of the houses. How shocked the ton would be to behold one of its most prominent members capering down the street, cold sober and in broad daylight, too! Therefore, he proceeded sedately, though he did, however, permit himself to whistle under his breath.

Then suddenly he stopped. His hand went to his side and he took out the list and smoothed it out. This time he studied it carefully and it was one item in particular which caused his straight brows to meet.

"Is it possible that, after all this, I have been mistaken?" In a considerably more chastened mood he continued on his way.

He did not wish to jump to conclusions, but only one lady of his acquaintance was addicted to list-making and she had been in his phaeton yesterday. He had thought he now understood the situation, but again he had clearly underestimated Miss Neville. After all, how else could one interpret that very unambiguous notation: "Célie's—wedding clothes"?

When he reached Agincourt Circle, signs of unusual activity greeted him. A travelling chaise had drawn up in front of number twenty-five; liveried footmen were busily unloading a series of boxes and baggages.

The front door stood open, but there was no sign of the butler or of other servants. Mr. Devereux stepped into the hall. Still no one appeared. He could hear raised voices from the interior of the house. With a slight shrug he made for them.

The noise led him to the morning room. Dev paused on the threshold and stared within. Slowly he raised his monocle.

Mrs. Cleeson lay back in a chintz-covered armchair. Beside her stood Ivor Devereux, alternatively fanning her and administering sal volatile. Before them, weeping copiously into her apron, huddled Emmie, Lucinda's maid. Next to her, staring rigidly ahead, his whole bearing registering deep affront, was the Neville butler. A little removed from this group, leaning on the mantelpiece with one booted foot resting on the new, polished steel fender, Jasper Neville sardonically surveyed his cousin and retainers.

Richard was slightly acquainted with Jasper and it was to him that he spoke. "Your pardon, sir. I would not intrude, but . . ."

Mrs. Cleeson sat up and shrieked at the sound of his voice. She clutched convulsively at Ivor's sleeve. "Mr. Devereux! He can tell you, Jasper, that we none of us had the slightest idea that any such action was—"

"Pray calm yourself, Ethelreda," Jasper replied. "No reproach whatever is due you, I am sure of that."

At this response, Dev's mouth tightened. "If it is not too great an impertinence, may I enquire—"

"Eloped!" Mrs. Cleeson released Ivor's coat and pressed a hand to her heart. "This very morning. Who could have guessed it?"

Dev's mouth became a thin, hard line. Here was the obvious explanation of the note in his pocket. "In that case I am decidedly *de trop*. I must—"

Jasper raised his hand. "If we may detain you, Mr. Devereux. I believe that you were present during these rather melodramatic events at Vauxhall last night?"

"Some of them." Dev's expression did not change.

"And you saw them." Mrs. Cleeson moaned and fell back farther into her chair. "But why? Why should they take this way? Why Gretna Green? Who could have objected to this match?"

"Dash it all, Ethelreda," Ivor complained as he applied the smelling salts. "So the gel faints. She seems to make a habit of it, don't she? But anyhow this time she chooses young Ryland to catch her, not Ricky. But it don't mean she has to elope with him, do it?"

"Precisely." Jasper took out his snuffbox. "There is no need for Lucinda to elope. I am trying to discover just why such a notion should enter my cousin's head."

"What else should I think?" demanded Mrs. Cleeson. "I have suspected a growing tendre, for they were much in each other's company." She inhaled deeply of the salts. "But, you know, I had begun to think that after all . . ." Her voice trailed off.

"Yes, Ethelreda?" Jasper prompted patiently, "you had began to think . . ."

Mrs. Cleeson cast a quick glance up at Richard and then looked away. "But that can scarcely signify now, for I am obviously proved wrong. They met clandestinely last night to plan the elopement. I had no idea till I learned that she had vanished without a word to anyone."

"If I may be allowed to speak, madam," said the butler, coming reluctantly to life, "Miss Neville ordered her coach and footman to be brought round shortly before eleven this morning."

"An unusual proceeding for an elopement," Jasper commented, opening his snuffbox.

"If I might put a question . . ." Mr. Devereux's face had been losing its set look and a certain suspicion was beginning to take shape in his mind. "Did Miss Neville receive any callers this morning?"

"No, sir," the butler replied. "That is to say, there was a caller, but she was not received. She was in haste, so she said, and merely left a letter for Miss Neville. I gave it—" he sniffed audibly "—to that young person over there." He nodded at Emmie.

Emmie's first response was to howl louder than ever, but for a moment, no one paid any attention to her.

"Was this caller," Mr. Devereux asked, raising his voice, "by any chance Miss Belle Ryland?"

"It was, sir."

"Now, see here, gel," Ivor said sharply to Emmie, "stop this infernal snivelling and tell us about this dashed letter."

"I don't know what it was, sir. Miss didn't show it to me, or tell me what it said. She just put it in her reticule and told me to have the carriage brought round."

"And it was after she read this letter that she ordered the carriage?"

"Yes, sir."

"Dashed if I see how that helps, anyway," said Ivor, dissatisfied. "Gels elopin' leave letters. They don't *get* 'em."

"Absolutely correct, my dear uncle." Richard smiled at him. "As usual, you have hit it in the ring."

"Aha, Ricky, my boy. Do you see something in all this?"

"What *I* see," said Jasper tartly, "is that girls eloping do not commonly do so in their chaise, attended by their own footman and without a single piece of luggage."

"But if she is not eloping, what is she doing?" Mrs. Cleeson demanded distractedly. "Where is she now?"

Jasper tranquilly took snuff. "Lucinda is not a fool, though," he remarked meditatively, his eyes meeting Dev's, "that is not to say that she does not, like the rest of us, occasionally behave foolishly."

Dev held Jasper's gaze. "Sir, I assure you this question is not mere vulgar curiosity, but is your daughter engaged?"

Jasper looked thoughtfully into his snuffbox. He snapped it shut. "No," he said.

"Then I must take my leave of you all." The Beau made his famous bow. "This has been a most instructive morning."

Jasper spoke to the butler, "Have a horse saddled and brought round for Mr. Devereux."

"But, Ricky, how the deuce will you find her?"

"I suspect there has been, shall we say, a hitch in the arrangements. An elopement was the intended impression, all right."

"I knew it! I knew it!" Mrs. Cleeson moaned again and Emmie's sobs increased in volume.

"The Great North Road," Jasper muttered, with a nod at Dev. "It will have taken them some time to cross London. You will be quicker on horseback."

"I'm desolate to leave you, Ivor, in such demanding circumstances." Mr. Devereux looked mischievously at Mrs. Cleeson and Emmie. "But I am sure you will contrive. Incidentally—" his smile grew and he took out the fatal list "—I believe this concerns you rather more than me." Picking up his gloves, he turned to Jasper, saying, "I trust we shall presently better our acquaintanceship, sir."

"I don't doubt it," Jasper replied.

CHAPTER SIXTEEN

THE COACH BOUNCED and jolted. Lucinda closed her eyes and held firmly to the straps. "I shall not be sick," she muttered to herself, *"I shall not."*

But she had scarcely slept the previous night and she had left without breakfast that morning. A throbbing pain cut through her head and waves of nausea swept over her. Despite her hold, she swayed sickeningly with every movement of the coach.

She tried to fix her mind on the object of this terrible journey. Belle and Miles Stratton? She had thought that affair ended at Lucy Caldeane's. She should have told someone she had seen them at the balloon ascent. There must have been something she could have done to avert this outcome.

Belle must be truly bewitched to elope in such a way. Nothing could lessen such a scandal. *Even if my own life is irretrievably ruined,* thought Lucinda, *I must stop Belle from ruining hers.*

And what about Sir Charles? Under all his posturing, he loved Belle and she had thought Belle loved him. How would he feel when the news of this flight burst upon him?

Just as I felt, Lucinda answered her own question. *Just as I felt when I found that brooch.* A tear trickled down her cheek and she brushed it impatiently away. She must stop thinking of Richard Devereux. He was going to marry Lady Chloris dePoer and she—she was going to marry Will Ryland.

With a sob, Lucinda recalled that morning in the orchard—so long ago now it seemed. What was it she had said then? "Everything will be the same." More tears ran down her face, but she did not heed them.

Now, nothing could ever be the same. Now she had come to London and met Richard Devereux. Too late she had learned that Papa was right. Love was more than the kindly affection she felt for Will.

But, Lucinda thought, she was glad to have known the other kind, however briefly, however much pain it brought. That was the kind of love Papa had meant, that was the enduring joy and consolation he had mentioned.

A lump rose in her throat as she thought of Papa; Papa who had fixed so many things before, healed so many hurts. But she was grown up now. Papa could not mend a broken heart.

She groped blindly for the handkerchief. In the driver's seat, Albert shouted and the coach lurched forward. Lucinda uttered a little shriek and grasped the strap again. Then she heard hoof-beats racing towards them.

She felt a stab of fear. Could it be highwaymen? But surely not on an open highway, in full daylight?

The hoof-beats thundered closer as the rider gained on them. A streak of black flashed past the window. Albert was shouting again. The coach swung to one side and bounced to a stop.

Lucinda heard running footsteps, the door was wrenched open and then—

"Mr. Devereux!" Lucinda gasped, rising to her feet. "Richard," she called, stretching her hands out to him, "Richard!"

"Lucinda, watch out!" But his warning came too late. Lucinda's forehead sharply contacted the top of the door. A shower of coloured lights burst before her eyes, and for the second time in their acquaintance, she fainted in Beau Devereux's arms.

SHE AWAKENED to the sound of bird-song. A gentle breeze cooled her cheeks and stirred her curls. She was comfortably lying down and she could smell briar-roses.

She opened her eyes to stare up at a lacy panoply of green leaves and then, directly above her, into a pair of clear grey eyes. Her head was in Mr. Devereux's lap.

"No, don't get up," he ordered gently. "We've pulled off, down a side lane. You gave yourself quite a knock, you know. I'm afraid you will have rather a bruise and you may still be feeling somewhat unwell from carriage sickness."

"I overheard you in Hatchard's. You didn't believe that I had carriage sickness then."

"You overheard me, did you? So that accounts for your freezing me out at Lady Grantham's. I didn't thaw for three days."

There was a look in those grey eyes that made Lucinda's pulse race. She glanced away and suddenly cried out. "Good heavens! Belle! I had forgot Belle!" She struggled to rise.

"Rest easy, my dear." Dev pushed her gently back.

"But you don't understand! Belle—"

"I understand perfectly and I urge you to go on forgetting your troublesome friend. Belle is not eloping."

"But she wrote to me. She and Miles Stratton, early this morning..."

"I thought it must be something like that," said Mr. Devereux with satisfaction. "I am becoming rather an expert on Miss Ryland's machinations. I can assure you that she is safely at home. When I last saw her, scarce three hours ago, she and Charles were planning a cosy tête-à-tête. If he's got any sense, he'll take a horsewhip to her, but I suspect he's doing something quite different."

His calm tones carried conviction, and Lucinda allowed herself to relax again. It was all so deliciously comfortable. Like a dream, really, or like coming home after a long journey. "But if Belle is really going to marry Charles, why should she send me such a letter?"

"That, my love, was her second line of defence, as it were."

It added enormously to Lucinda's well-being to hear him say "my love" and her flush deepened at his caressing tone.

"What I should like to know," he continued, "is how I was to be informed where you were, so that I might gallantly ride after you. What exactly did Miss Ryland tell you to do?"

"Tell no one but Emmie."

"She knew you would try to go after her but what she didn't know was that you, ever the soul of discretion, decided not to risk telling even your maid. Off you went then, as she had planned, but without leaving the clue she was depending on. Fortunately, my understanding of Miss Ryland has progressed considerably since I first met her."

Lucinda thought she could lie forever in that sun-lit glade, listening to that beloved voice. "What did you mean, her second line?"

"Vauxhall was her first. I suspect I was to rescue you from her attentions as that singularly unconvincing young man. She would run away, boots permitting, of course. You would fall gratefully into my arms and we would admit our mutual passion. Young Ryland was the joker in that pack."

"Will!" Lucinda sat bolt upright. "I can't! I mustn't! I'm to marry Will!"

"You must please yourself, my love. But I fancy Ryland will draw the line at bigamy."

"Bi-bigamy?"

"How pleased Lady Grantham must be to have both her children turned off in the same Season—and to members of the same family, too."

"Do you mean Will and *Patience?*"

Dev lifted a mahogany curl and twisted it round his finger. His touch electrified her, as did his words. "You know, Lucinda, I cannot decide whether you are more beautiful in sunlight or candlelight. However, I intend to take a whole lifetime to study the question. Now let us clear away all misunderstandings."

Lucinda's heart was doing very strange things, but she was still astonished by Dev's revelation. "Patience and Will! I cannot..." She paused and then said, "But no. Now that you point it out, it seems very clear. And I never had the least inkling."

"Didn't you?" Richard gave her one of those deep, disturbing glances.

Her eyes dropped and she looked up at him through those long, dark lashes. "Do you mean I was too preoccupied with...with you?"

"Deplorably conceited as I am, I do."

"I was...worried about Lady Chloris." Lucinda spoke with a touch of constraint, but in this golden glade, with that light in Richard's eyes, Lady Chloris seemed very insubstantial.

"Ah, yes, Chloris. I must have been mad. I actually considered following my Aunt Melpond's advice. But then, one evening, a huge-eyed chit with chestnut hair fainted in my arms and nothing was ever the same again."

"Nothing was the same," Lucinda sighed in deepest satisfaction. "And the brooch?"

"Nothing to do with me. I had never seen it till you pushed it dramatically into my hand. I knew it wasn't mine, but I didn't know whose it was, and since you had told me you were promised to another, it didn't seem to matter."

Lucinda's hand stole out and tentatively touched one of Richard's. He captured it and held it firmly. "Did you ever discover to whom it did belong?"

"Not till this morning. Not Chloris and Richard, but Chloris and Rollo."

"Rollo? Who is that?"

"A prize young hothead, who also happens to be the Earl of Cranford."

"Cranford? But Papa said he was not in England."

"No one knew he was here. According to Chloris's rather incoherent note, he has been here in secret for some time."

"In secret? But why?"

Dev shrugged. "Three years ago there were rumours he and Chloris were a match. Then their fathers quarrelled. Rollo was only a younger son at the time. He went off to Italy and I should suppose they found some way to correspond. There was no enquiry about the brooch because no one was to know he had come back to England. He's the earl now and why they should choose to behave in such a havy-cavy—but then all the Cranfords have temperaments to match their hair."

"Red! I know. I glimpsed him at Almack's."

"I wish I had. It would have made many things clearer. In any event, there was indeed an elopement this morning. Cranford has got a special licence and they'll be married before they confront her parents. I suspect," said Dev with a touch of his old cynicism, "that they will find the opposition considerably lessened, now that Chloris is to be a countess. I'm grateful to her, though. She kept me from one of the biggest mistakes of my life. You must remind me, my love, we shall send them a magnificent wedding present."

For the past few minutes, Miss Neville had been experiencing an overwhelming desire to reach up and touch Mr. Devereux's face, just there, where the clean line of his jaw began. Greatly daring, she traced her finger along that path. When she reached his chin, Richard grasped the finger and brought it to his lips.

Then he gathered her to him. This time she locked her arms round his neck, lifted her face and closed her eyes. At last their lips met.

Much later, as they sat back against the tree, Lucinda nestled against him, in the crook of his arm, Dev said, "I see only one flaw in our otherwise perfect married life."

"My habit of fainting?" Lucinda said with her deep chuckle.

"Provided you confine yourself to fainting in my arms, I raise no objection. No, I refer to Miss Ryland. As Lady Grantham, she will be our near neighbour. The prospect terrifies me."

Lucinda laughed. "Let us hope she will be too busy with her own affairs." She looked thoughtful. "Does Patience have any money?"

Dev smiled down at her. "You have been in a world of your own, haven't you? The Granthams suffer no lack of juice."

"Good. I'm sure Will would marry Patience even if she were penniless, but I am glad she will be able to help him with his father's debts."

"I fancy he was beginning to make some order there, anyway. I rather suspect your father has been advising him. But Patience has, I believe, a substantial dowry and Charles will be generous in settlements." Dev dropped a kiss on the tip of Lucinda's nose and pulled her to her feet. "Speaking of your papa and settlements, I must get you back to him, before he thinks I've run off to Gretna Green with you myself."

"Couldn't you?" Lucinda looked teasingly at him.

"Don't tempt me, minx. Back into the coach with you and watch the door this time."

Mr. Devereux went back to the side of the lane. He woke Albert from a quiet snooze beneath a tree and saw to it that his mount was tethered behind the chaise. Then he came back to join Lucinda.

"Won't Papa be surprised when he hears?" asked Lucinda.

"I should very much doubt that anything can surprise your father. I imagine you probably told him more than you think in your letters, and my behaviour this morning made my own feelings obvious. Besides, he'll already have had one such announcement.''

''You mean Belle and Will?''

''No, I mean Ivor and Ethelreda.''

Lucinda chuckled. ''Now, that I did wonder about. I am so pleased for them.''

''I must warn you, though, I shall not consent to a double wedding!''

''How absurd you are, Richard. As if—'' The chaise jolted off along the bumpy side track. Lucinda's high spirits faded. ''You may not mind my fainting, but I cannot think you will like a wife who is constantly carriage sick.''

''But you are not going to be sick.''

''I'm not?''

''Certainly not. I shall sit beside you and every few minutes, I shall kiss you—like that—and you will not be sick.''

''And does that work?'' asked Lucinda demurely.

''Doctors recommend it as an infallible remedy.''

Whatever the extent of Mr. Devereux's medical knowledge, it was certainly true that Lucinda was not sick.

''In fact,'' she confided teasingly to Richard, as he helped her down, ''I think I might have enjoyed a longer journey.''

''Forward minx,'' said Dev reprovingly. Then he grinned. ''I shall take you to Beacon End, my house in Devon, for your honeymoon and that, my girl, is a very long journey.''

The Neville butler had not recovered his spirits in the interim. Lugubriously, he led them to the library where Jasper was waiting.

As Lucinda flew into her father's arms, Mr. Devereux said firmly, ''Sir, I wish to marry your daughter.''

''But of course,'' said Jasper.

Harlequin Intrigue®

QUID PRO QUO

Racketeer King Crawley is a man who lives by one rule: An Eye For An Eye. Put behind bars for his sins against humanity, Crawley is driven by an insatiable need to get even with the judge who betrayed him. And the only way to have his revenge is for the judge's children to suffer for their father's sins....

Harlequin Intrigue introduces Patricia Rosemoor's QUID PRO QUO series: #161 PUSHED TO THE LIMIT (May 1991), #163 SQUARING ACCOUNTS (June 1991) and #165 NO HOLDS BARRED (July 1991).

Meet:

Sydney Raferty: She is the first to feel the wrath of King Crawley's vengeance. Pushed to the brink of insanity, she must fight her way back to reality—with the help of Benno DeMartino in #161 PUSHED TO THE LIMIT.

Dakota Raferty: The judge's only son, he is a man whose honest nature falls prey to the racketeer's madness. With Honor Bright, he becomes an unsuspecting pawn in a game of deadly revenge in #163 SQUARING ACCOUNTS.

Asia Raferty: The youngest of the siblings, she is stalked by Crawley and must find a way to end the vendetta. Only one man can help—Dominic Crawley. But will the son join forces with his father's enemy in #165 NO HOLDS BARRED?

Don't miss a single title of Patricia Rosemoor's QUID PRO QUO trilogy coming to you from Harlequin Intrigue.

HARLEQUIN
Romance

**This June, travel to Turkey
with Harlequin Romance's**

THE JEWELS OF HELEN
by Jane Donnelly

She was a spoiled brat who liked her own way.

Eight years ago Max Torba thought Anni was self-centered—
and that she didn't care if her demands made life impossible
for those who loved her.

Now, meeting again at Max's home in Turkey, it was clear he
still held the same opinion, no matter how hard she tried to
make a good impression. "You haven't changed much, have
you?" he said. "You still don't give a damn for the trouble you
cause."

But did Max's opinion really matter? After all, Anni had no
intention of adding herself to his admiring band of female
followers....

Take 4 bestselling love stories FREE

Plus get a FREE surprise gift!

Back by Popular Demand

Janet Dailey
Americana

A romantic tour of America through fifty favorite Harlequin
Presents® novels, each set in a different state researched by
Janet and her husband, Bill. A journey of a lifetime in one
cherished collection.

In June, don't miss the sultry states featured in:

Title # 9 - **FLORIDA**
              Southern Nights
        #10 - **GEORGIA**
              Night of the Cotillion

Available wherever
Harlequin books are sold.

JD-JR